Other award-nominated novels by André Swartley:

THE ISLAND OF MISFIT TOYS[*]

AMERICANUS REX[**]

*Indiana Book Award Finalist

*Elliot Rosewater Booklist Nominee

**Next Generation Indie Book Awards Finalist

Published by Workplay Publishing
Bluffton, Ohio 45817
workplaypublishing.com

ISBN 0-9842122-5-6
Cover art, design and layout by André Swartley.

Characters, locations and events in this novel are products of the author's imagination or are used fictitiously. Resemblance to actual places, historical events or people, living or dead, is purely coincidental.

PRINTED IN THE UNITED STATES OF AMERICA

LEON MARTIN AND THE
FANTASY GIRL

LEON MARTIN AND THE

FANTASY GIRL

レオン・マーティンとファンタジーガール

A NOVEL

ANDRÉ SWARTLEY

work play
PUBLISHING

For Theresa and all of the other wonderful librarians in America's public schools

OPENING CINEMATIC

My hands were hurting again. It had started several hours ago, after our airplane had landed in Cologne. Initially I'd been able to bury the pain under the excitement of finally arriving in Germany but the humid ferry ride from Cologne down to St. Goar had only made the situation worse. Autumn had reveled in the balmy heat on the upper deck of the ferry, throwing back her long neck and letting the sun play across her face. I tolerated the heat for as long as I was able but in the end I retreated into the air conditioned main cabin. By that point I had lost too much fine motor control to dig the rigidly supportive Thermoskin gloves out of my backpack.

Autumn probably could have helped, but she still didn't know the extent of my arthritis—we had never really spoken during the single semester she attended New Canaan Mennonite High School—and I had no intention of allowing her to become my nurse on this trip. Certainly not on the first day. So when Autumn came down from the ferry's upper deck and asked how I was doing I put on a happy face.

Now I was paying the price. Despite the special zippers Mom installed on my backpack—supposedly even easier to operate than Velcro—I still hadn't managed to open the pocket containing my gloves, and the pain was growing worse by the minute. I reasoned that a long exploratory walk through my new hometown might at least tire me out so I could sleep all night and start fresh tomorrow but the heavy, humid air was crushing my bones like a giant's handshake.

Still, I'd made it. No more troubled frowns from Dr. Elmore whenever the subject of traveling to Germany came up, no more anxious suggestions from my mother that the money I'd saved for this trip could just as easily go into my college fund.

Now that I was in my German hometown for the summer, celebrating my first evening here with a walk along the river, there could be no question that I'd made the correct choice. Scenery like this might exist in Iowa but I'd certainly never encountered it. A castle, stern and brilliant in the glare of yellow ghost lights, stood on a cliff overlooking the town. Half a block to the northeast dark water sloshed against the muddy bank of the Rhine River. An ancient tanker lumbered southward on the current, visible only as a bulky shadow against the yellow glow of streetlamps across the river. The valley was narrow here, and the night still enough that I could hear the tanker's wake lapping at the opposite shore.

"*Guten Abend,*" said an elderly gentleman pleasantly as I passed. He was sitting on a bench in the circular glow of a streetlamp. He clutched the bend of his cane in an enviably firm grip.

Before I could return his greeting a sharp, high, clearly feminine cry echoed through the still air and died out over the river. I told myself I didn't recognize the voice that had made that sound. Autumn had mentioned that she might take a walk too but…

Please, not on our first night in Germany.

The old man resettled himself on the bench and grimaced distastefully in the direction from which the cry had come. He rattled off some haughty sounding German that I might have understood in different circumstances, but with the cry still fading in my ears I heard mostly gibberish.

I did pick out a single term which I repeated as a question. *"Die Kneipe?"*

This wasn't vocabulary Mrs. Miller had spent much time explaining in German class, though she had admitted, "Beer is an important part of German culture. Many Germans of all ages visit a *Biergarten* or *Kneipe*, which we might call bars or pubs, in the evenings for a social drink with their friends."

Nothing perks up a classroom of Mennonite teenagers like the mention of alcohol.

"Ja, natürlich die Kneipe," the old man repeated in a deep, pursed tone of disapproval.

Another shout rang down the street, this time followed by a rush of loud, harsh laughter.

"Thanks," I said to the old man, starting to run. *"Danke,* I mean. Sorry."

He called after me. I didn't bother to translate. Every footfall on the uneven cobbled street brought a quick, ringing jolt like a hammer blow through my knuckles up to my elbows. Sort of rocking from heel to toe as I ran seemed to help a little but after a short distance constant pain began to roll up and down my forearms like molten ball bearings.

I heard jukebox music now, faint beneath the rasp of my own breath in my ears. More laughter. Wouldn't I feel silly if I burst into the *Kneipe*, gasping like a hooked perch, only to find a bunch of strangers playing some drinking game, clapping, laughing, and hollering along to the music?

I followed the noise around a corner into a little alley. Eight feet up on the outer wall of the building on the left was a discreet sign reading Flußgasse. River Street, or something like that. I remembered Mrs. Miller telling us the word *Gasse* didn't translate very well into English and referred to a narrow pathway of some kind. Now that I was pelting down the center of one at full speed, however, I thought it just looked like a regular old alley. Why did teachers always act like the stuff they taught was so darned complica—

A tinkle of breaking glass rippled through the alleyway. The jukebox music stopped suddenly, as did the laughter. Uneasy voices drifted from a lighted doorway and bank of windows half a block ahead. Several Germans sitting at the round tables outside the *Kneipe*'s front windows stopped their conversations and peered inside with obvious concern.

I reached the doorway and pushed through with my right shoulder, sending a new river of fire down that arm. In the dim haze of the *Kneipe* I could make out heavy wooden tables running the room's full length. All along the back wall enormous barrels were stacked like a medieval king's supply of mead. To my right stood a high bar packed with an impossible amount of exotic bottles.

But these things were mere periphery. All eyes in the *Kneipe* were on two people in the middle of the room, one of whom was Autumn. Sometime between now and the supper we'd eaten with our host parents she'd changed out of her travel clothes into a tight blue halter top and khaki shorts that showed more leg than my mother's bathing suit.

She stood red faced before an absolutely hulking German man of perhaps twenty-five. He was well over six feet tall, shaved bald and covered in bulging, trembling muscles. He wore a gold ring in his nose and looked like nothing so much as a bull that had learned to stand on its hind legs.

Autumn brandished the top half of a brown beer bottle that ended in a spiky cylinder just below the neck. Judging from the yellow spatters on the guy's white t-shirt the bottle had been full when Autumn had broken it and started taking swings at him.

"*Nochmal ein Flittchen aus dem Internet,*" the bull sneered to his friend. "*Dieses hat größere Titten, oder?*"

14

He made a suggestive squeezing motion. His thick hands and forearms were covered in angry little red dots that might have been bug bites or healing injuries from previous bar fights. Or needle tracks, I supposed. Lord knew the guy was big enough to be using steroids, and the thickest cluster of marks was visible near his elbow, where drug addicts in movies usually juiced up.

"If you touch me again," Autumn raged up into his red face, "we'll see how many of those big squirmy veins I have to cut open before you pass out." She puckered her mouth and gobbed a lace of spit onto his cheek.

One of the veins Autumn had mentioned pulsed in his forehead. "*Schlampe*," he spat softly.

Although I didn't know that particular word its many possible meanings were evident. I stepped fully into the *Kneipe* without any idea of what I meant to do.

"*Guten Abend!*" I shouted, trying to sound as cheerful as possible. Everyone's attention shifted to me. So far so good. "*Bitte, dieses Mädchen ist meine Schwester,*" I adlibbed.

It was a bad lie. Autumn and I couldn't have looked less like brother and sister. She was short and powerful with legs like a field hockey player whereas ever since my growth spurt last summer my body had the general shape and muscle definition of a wooden spoon. But I also didn't think anyone would be paying close attention at the moment.

I searched my memory for the German word for "crazy" and after a moment I found it. "*Sie ist verrückt,*" I explained. When that didn't seem to connect with my audience I pointed dramatically to the side of my head. "*Im Kopf!*"

Some of the tension began to ebb from the room. Muted chuckles erupted at a table to my left. Even if these were at the expense of my German, just hearing them lightened my heart.

"Leon, what are you doing here?" Autumn asked. She sounded nonchalant, annoyed even, that I had busted up her evening.

"We're going home. Our host parents will be wor—"

The body builder clamped a beefy hand around Autumn's fingers and the neck of the beer bottle. He jerked up on her arm and she staggered toward him, off balance. A second more powerful jerk lifted Autumn off her feet, arm extended awkwardly over her head.

Before I even knew I had moved I was standing between Autumn and the bald giant, shoving them apart and sending splintery, aching heat through my unprotected knuckles and wrists.

I may as well have been shoving at a redwood tree. Unperturbed, the giant yanked again on the bottle, this time pulling down instead of up. It slipped out of Autumn's grip at last and suddenly jagged glass was slicing through the air toward my face, glistening beads of beer still clinging to the sharp edges like saliva on pointed teeth.

I had time to register surprise on the guy's face. His arm shifted strangely as if he might be trying to stop his downward stroke but it was too late. New, stinging pain lanced down the center of my forehead and I went to my knees with the force of it.

A hot wet stripe ran from my forehead down the bridge of my nose and dripped between my lips. It tickled. I thought about wiping it away, but my hands hurt for some reason.

Autumn might have screamed my name, but I was quite occupied with the shiny red drops appearing on the toes of the big German guy's dress shoes. The shoes looked expensive. Why was he letting beer drip all over them?

Wait, was German beer red?

It was all terribly confusing and truth be told I didn't want to think about it anymore. I thought I might feel better if I went to sleep for a while. So that's what I did.

DISC 1

1

Warm breeze blew through the skylight above my bed, ruffling the sheer white curtains. My room was bright, meaning the sun had already come up…

Except this wasn't my room. I tried to sit up and didn't make it very far. My forehead felt like it might split open. My eyes throbbed and I squeezed them shut against a wave of nausea.

All of this began to make sense as I woke more fully. My room looked different because I was in Germany. This room with the skylight and white curtains would be my room for the rest of the summer. The unyielding futon under my body would be my bed. I attempted to look around again and discovered my eyes didn't open very far. A tuft of white on the inner periphery of my vision reminded me vaguely of a confused rush to the hospital last night with my new host father. Which further reminded me that my host mother had said she would serve breakfast at 8:00.

That I could remember these things must surely be a good sign. No permanent brain damage or anything. Of course, I thought dryly, someone whose brain had been damaged probably wouldn't be able to realize it.

I twisted my head to the right to check the travel alarm clock I'd set up by my bed when I'd unpacked yesterday afternoon. The little clock had fallen over at some point in the night. I reached over to right it and that's when I saw the jumbled knot of knuckles my hand had become overnight. Suddenly the pain in my head fell to a distant second place.

What had I done after my host father had brought me back from the hospital last night? I couldn't remember. My clothes were in a pile on the floor, but the special pocket on my backpack was still zipped tight, the Thermoskin gloves trapped uselessly inside. I wondered how easily I could open that pocket with my teeth.

Someone knocked on the door. I tried to say "Just a second" but only managed a dismayed croak. The doorknob twisted and Autumn stepped into the room, forehead creased with concern.

"How do you feel?"

I cleared my throat. "My head hurts."

"Do you remember anything? What's your name?"

I attempted a smile. "Typhoon Darkwater."

Her eyes flashed the poisonous green of a tropical snake. "Goddammit, Leon, I'm not kidding around here. You have fifteen stitches in your forehead."

"Please don't say that word. I'm fine."

She calmed herself. "What's my name?"

"Autumn." I struggled to sit up again without letting my bunched hands come into contact with anything besides the air, every molecule of which seemed to be rocketing around the room and slamming into my hands and forehead like a fifty-pound cannonball. "We just graduated from New Canaan Mennonite High School and we're on a summer service trip in Germany in a small town called St. Goar. Our host parents are named Klaus and Greta and they are undoubtedly downstairs waiting for us to come to breakfast. How's that? Do I pass the test?"

Autumn sighed in relief and wrapped her fingers gently around mine. I tried not to scream.

"Can you please get my support gloves?" I said. "They're in the front pocket of my backpack."

She unzipped the pocket with thoughtless ease and drew out the black gloves. I rarely wore them at school because I could tell my classmates and teachers had to work very hard to ignore them. Not Autumn, though. On the airplane as I had struggled into my gloves before attempting to sleep for a few hours she had surprised me with a joke that I must go to a lot of biker bars if I owned gloves like that. At that moment I thought I'd never seen a more beautiful girl.

I hadn't told her that, of course. She probably thought I was enough of a weirdo already.

"Left one first?" she asked now. I nodded. Her eyebrows knitted as she looked helplessly at the gnarled tree roots my hands had become while I'd slept. "How do I…?"

"You just kind of rub them until my fingers open." My cheeks burned with humiliation. So much for Autumn not becoming my nurse. "Not too fast."

Autumn began slowly unbinding my left fist, chatting as she did so. "The police came to the bar and arrested that bodybuilder asshole last night. I had to stay and give them a statement about what happened. That's why I didn't go to the hospital with you and Klaus. I didn't understand everything the cops said, but I had the distinct feeling they recognized our friend Johann von Beefcake. Maybe he's taken a swing at somebody before." She smiled wryly. "The bartender apologized to me up and down. I got the idea he wasn't anxious to lose the income from two American teenagers for a whole summer. I didn't have the heart to tell him you don't drink."

She had coaxed enough of the familiar packed cotton and broken glass feeling from my knuckles to slide my left hand into the glove.

"I like how your little fingertips stick out the ends," she said. "It's cute."

When she let go my hand wanted to curl up again but the rigid glove held it open.

Two years, I thought. *Two years of arthritis and it already feels like my whole life. What will my hands look and feel like when I'm sixty? Heck, when I'm thirty.*

Autumn moved to the other side of my bed and started on my other hand. "Leon?" She was leaning forward over my hand, her hair a golden curtain over a cheek that had suddenly reddened. "What you did for me last night was really great. There aren't too many boys who would stand up for me the way you did, especially to a brute like that."

I didn't know what to say. It wasn't like I had made a conscious choice last night. In fact, this morning I only remembered the incident in stark images like flash-pictures: the golden glint of the bald giant's nose ring; the shiny streak of Autumn's spit sliding down his flushed cheek; the jerking motion of his arm and the whisper of movement as the beer bottle swung downward toward my face.

"I would have done the same for anyone," I said.

Her fingers stopped moving against mine for the briefest moment then resumed. "Well," she said, "you did it for me last night and I appreciate it."

"You're welcome."

She worked another minute in silence before she was able to slide the right glove over my hand and tighten the wrist strap. "Better?"

"Thank you," I said. "What started it between you and that guy last night anyway?"

"You mean what did he do that made me go all slasher-movie?" Autumn rolled her eyes. "The usual. He recognized me from my website and thought it entitled him to a grope. My dad would probably agree with him," she muttered.

"Wait, you mean your dad—"

"No," she interrupted firmly. "Jerry's never touched me like that. He's not that big of a butthole. But he did suggest that the pictures on my site would give men everywhere an excuse to try to rape me or whatever."

She adopted the straight necked posture I was already learning to associate with her imitation of her father. "'Autumn, men can't always tell the difference between their desires and reality, so you shouldn't tempt them if you don't want the wrong kind of attention.'"

"Okay, but—" I began.

"That still doesn't explain why I tried to cut the guy's face off, right?" Autumn shook her head. "Loads of guys have tried to pick me up or feel me up, even before I started the website. But this one was different."

"Yeah, talk about roid rage."

She shook her head again but before she could elaborate another knock came at the door. Greta, our host mother, stuck her head inside the room. She had not bodily crossed the threshold of my room since I'd moved in. If not for her fingers visibly balancing her weight against the door frame she might have been only a floating head with cropped, stark white hair.

"*Frühstück,*" Greta announced, frowning first at the long, wide strip of gauze taped to my forehead, then even more deeply at my gloves. "*Willst du im Bett essen?*"

"*Nein, danke,*" I said at once. I wasn't going to make her serve me breakfast in bed, especially if entering my room made her uncomfortable. Greta nodded smartly. Her head floated back out of the doorway.

"*Frühstück* is breakfast, right?" Autumn asked.

"Breakfast," I agreed. "It literally means 'early piece,' if that helps you remember."

"It doesn't. Do you need help getting dressed or anything?"

An image flashed into my head of Autumn leaning over in front of me, pulling up my pants like I was toddler whose diaper she had just changed. Compared to such mortification I suddenly thought spontaneous combustion might not be such a bad way to go. Autumn, however, didn't seem embarrassed at all.

"That's—" My voice cracked. "That's generous of you but all my shirts are pullovers and all my pants are either elastic or Velcro. Thanks again for your help with the gloves though."

Autumn shrugged. "I would have done the same for anyone."

2

Klaus and Greta's kitchen lay at the bottom of a treacherously narrow and steep staircase that led down from the hallway between Autumn's and my rooms. I did my best to navigate the narrow stairs without using the handrail—I'd managed to dress myself but at the moment I would rather have fallen down ten flights of stairs than have to use my hands for anything else.

"Good morning, *meine Lieben!*" Klaus boomed from the head of the breakfast table.

With his neatly groomed white beard—*sans* mustache like the Amish men who tended the farmland around New Canaan—and his plump, permanently rosy cheeks he reminded me strongly of a garden gnome.

Greta blew air through her teeth in a prim, disapproving chirp. "*Deutsch, Kläuschen,*" she reminded him. She, at least, had read the service program rules that we were supposed to speak only German in our host homes.

Klaus heeded his wife and spoke in German but only to remind her that "the girl," as he called Autumn, spoke less German than a typical hedgehog and it would be impolite not to include her in the morning's conversation. His sense of politeness apparently did not preclude criticizing Autumn's language abilities in her presence. And anyway he was right. Oblivious, Autumn turned to me, trying not to laugh. "They're so cute."

"My wife tells me not to speak the English, yes?" Klaus said cheerfully. His mirth faded as he took in my bruises and bandages. "Are you certain you can meet with Frau Werner today? The church is fifteen minutes away on foot. I can also take you by car on my way to work."

Klaus's driving was one of the few things I remembered clearly from last night. I'd rather have gone another round with the bodybuilder guy than get in a car with him again but I didn't say so. "*Danke, aber ich kann gern laufen. Ich habe nur Kopfschmerzen.*"

Greta beamed at me for returning the conversation to German.

"He has a headache, yes?" Klaus translated for Autumn, earning another chirp from his wife. "In that case I will talk more quietly."

This must have been a joke because his considerable belly shook against the table, nearly toppling the softboiled egg from the porcelain stand on his placemat. Greta deposited a warm roll on each of our plates. Klaus expertly tore his in two and spread a thick layer of butter and a pinch of chives on each half.

Autumn wordlessly cut my roll and garnished one half with white cheese and the other with a slice of hard salami. "Thanks." She nodded.

"What will you be doing after Frau Werner gives your service assignments?" Klaus went on. "I think the assignments do not begin until tomorrow."

"I'd like to see more of the town," Autumn said. "Are there walking paths by the river?"

"*Ja, ja,*" Klaus said around a mouthful of bread and chives. "Places to walk all over St. Goar. Castles and vineyards. Very beautiful."

"*Was?*" Greta asked.

"*Die Kinder möchten entlang den Rhein laufen,*" Klaus translated loudly.

"*Nimm die Autumn mit,*" Greta warned me.

"What'd she say?" Autumn asked, obviously recognizing her name.

All this translating was going to get old fast. "She says if we go walking I should take you with me."

I could see Autumn gearing up for an argument. Her body language was so clear she might as well have spoken aloud: *I don't need anyone to protect me.* She seemed to have forgotten how doe-eyed she had become twenty minutes ago about me stepping between her and that Neanderthal.

"I don't think we'll have time to go walking anyway," I told her. "Our schedule says there's food and a mixer to meet the other student volunteers after we get our assignments."

"Oh yeah." Autumn pursed her lips in distaste.

"Look, I'll just stick close to you until you get the hang of speaking German," I said. "After that I'll leave you alone. I'm sure you'll find better things to do than watch me fuss with my gloves for three months."

"It's not that," she said quickly.

"Or," I said, "if you want to see the town, why don't you bring your guidebook to the church, and after the mixer we'll see how much of St. Goar we can fit in before supper. I can even help you with your German if you want."

She leveled a calculating gaze at me. I tried not to squirm.

"Leon Martin, peacemaker," she said.

For the first time today I smiled for real. "I'm Mennonite. It's what we do."

At last Greta sat down with the rest of us and gave grace in German even though we had already started eating. After the blessing, Klaus regaled us about German food and culture without cease, neither requiring nor apparently desiring us to contribute anything to the conversation. Greta returned to her feet after only a few bites and began packing clear plastic bags with our lunch: two sandwiches, a juice box, and an unfamiliar type of granola bar. These she handed to Autumn, who stuffed both lunches into her backpack with a self-conscious murmur of "*Danke.*"

"Go, my children!" Klaus bellowed as we stood from the table. "You will return for the evening meal, yes?"

We promised we would.

"And you will come back if you feel too much pain?" he added, eyeing me severely.

"*Natürlich. Bitte haben Sie keine Angst,*" I said confidently, earning another warm smile from Greta.

She stood on her tiptoes and gave Autumn and me a quick, dry kiss on the cheek before herding us out the door. Last night in the darkness and humidity St. Goar had felt cozy and small, but sunlight threw the valley wide open. Hills too big to be called hills and too small to be called mountains rose to the north, south, and west as if the town were being cradled in a giant's cupped palms. As soon as our feet hit the sidewalk, Autumn pointed up at a ruined old castle high above town, seemingly carved into the side of the smaller, closer hill. It was the same one I had noticed last night.

"What is that place?" Without waiting for an answer she whipped her guidebook out of her backpack. "It's called Burg Rheinfels," she declared, running her finger along a line of text. "It used to be the largest castle on the Rhine. We can tour the grounds for under five Euros."

"You sure are excited to see the town," I said, trying not to sound too surprised. Autumn's reputation at school hadn't exactly suggested an interest in geography or history.

"Do you know where Mom and Jerry used to take me on vacation before they got divorced?" she said distractedly. "Disneyland. Every year, literally since I can remember. We didn't visit the rest of

Los Angeles or even Anaheim. Just Disneyland for one week every freaking year. God, I've never even been to Des Moines."

"Please don't say that," I said before I could stop myself.

"What, Des Moines?" she asked innocently.

I felt my cheeks redden. "Sorry. Using the Lord's name in vain has always been the ultimate no-no in my home. Shouting the f-word at my grandmother would probably get me in less trouble than that."

Autumn was appraising me again. I wasn't sure I could stand three months of that look.

"Don't apologize," she finally said. "If it's important to you I'll try to stop. Anyway, I don't want to piss you off before I see if any others students in the program are worth knowing."

"That's sensible."

She sighed, sounding annoyed again. What was with this girl? Keeping track of her emotions was like riding a rollercoaster in the dark. Like riding Space Mountain at Disneyland, in fact. Was that the kind of joke you could tell a girl?

"Did something funny just happen in that little head of yours, Leon?" Autumn asked, smiling a little herself. "For the record I won't ditch you no matter how cool the other students are. The outcasts of New Canaan Mennonite High School should stick together even if we've already graduated, right?"

And with that I realized Autumn and I actually had something in common.

3

The St. Goar *Mennoniten-Kirche* disappointingly resembled most Mennonite churches in Iowa: low, drab, and brown. The outer walls were stone rather than wood or the ghastly corrugated steel that wove in and out of fashion every few years in the Midwest, but after seeing the Catholic cathedral in Cologne I had been hoping to worship in a more impressive church for the summer.

"There's something to be said for familiarity I guess," I said to Autumn.

She shrugged. "I haven't gone to church since Mom and Jerry split up. It's one reason he sent me to New Canaan high. You know, give me to the Mennonites to save my soul or whatever."

The church's front doors were made of heavy, dark wood. A square of poster board had been taped to one of the doors. Written on it in black magic marker were the words, *Amerikanische Studenten, Willkommen in St. Goar!* At the bottom of the poster was another message, scribbled in English almost as an afterthought: *Cake and punch inside.*

"They went all out with that sign, didn't they?" Autum said dryly. "Maybe this will make up for the senior prom we never got."

"That's another Mennonite thing…" I began.

"I know, I know. Dancing leads to premarital sex. I got the memo." Autumn cocked her elbow formally. "Leon, I would be honored to be your date to this mixer."

A little flutter went through my belly but I ignored it. She was only joking, after all. Girls like Autumn didn't go for guys like me. And besides that there was the matter of her website.

My mother's response when she'd heard Autumn would be traveling to Germany with me had been atypically severe: "Leon, there's a reason boys want to go with girls who look like Autumn Springer and it's the same reason mothers don't want their sons with them. Please trust me when I say you wouldn't want to marry anyone who had already done the things she's done."

She had then hesitated before uttering what was probably the most damning statement she could think to make about Autumn: "Girls like Autumn Springer only know one way to interact with boys."

"Yo!" Autumn snapped her fingers in front of my eyes. "Prom date. We going inside?"

"Okay," I said awkwardly. I pulled open the big wooden door for her, pleased I could do it so easily. The handle was nice and thick and my hands were feeling noticeably better after an hour inside the support gloves.

Autumn inclined her head and swept regally forward but stopped short almost immediately. A mountainously tall woman of about forty with a severe helmet of steely blond hair had appeared as soon as I'd opened the door. She passed through the church's high front doors without ducking, but not by much.

"Good morning, I—" she began in lightly accented English. Then she saw the bandages on my face. "*Mein Gott,* do you need to see a doctor?"

I smiled as convincingly as I could. The medical tape holding the bandage to my forehead pulled against my cheeks and scalp. "I had an accident last night. Klaus Holz already took me to the doctor."

"*Ach so,* you are the young man staying with the Holzes." Her eyes flashed down to my gloves and back up to my face almost too quickly to notice. Almost.

"Leon Martin," I confirmed.

"Yes, forgive my ill manners. I am called Anna Werner. I direct the Culture of Service training program in Nordrhein-Westfalen, Hessen, Rheinland-Pfalz, and Saarland."

After Autumn introduced herself Frau Werner led us through a dim hallway with a plaster ceiling so low that she had to walk with her head stooped. Soon we came to a small room with rows of folding chairs against three of the walls. A table covered in white linen was set up against the room's fourth wall. As promised, two cakes had been laid out for us, a chocolate upside-down cake and a creamy cheesecake with what looked like dried apricots on top. Several glass bottles of something called Mezzo Mix completed the buffet.

Two other American students were inside the room already. The guy had a broad chest and an unconvincing goatee (though it was admittedly better than anything I could have grown myself). The girl was dark haired and cute but so skinny she looked like she would need to eat both of the cakes by herself to achieve an appropriate weight for her height.

"Leon Martin and Autumn Springer," Frau Werner introduced us. "This is Ronald Hatfield and Elise Yoder. They arrived in St. Goar early this morning."

The four of us exchanged awkward greetings before Frau Werner excused herself to wait for the remaining student.

"Well," I said, sitting down in the folding chair just inside the door. "So where are you guys from?"

"Dude, what happened to your face?" Ronald Hatfield asked. "You get in a bar fight or something?"

"Something like that," I said, trying to sound sarcastic. I had no interest in explaining last night's events. And anyway I doubted Autumn would want these strangers to know that a drunken German had tried to feel her up because he'd seen her naked on the internet.

Ronald wasn't paying attention to me anyway. He was staring at Autumn with an expression that said he couldn't believe his luck. I could almost hear his thoughts: *Three months trapped in a small town in Germany with a girl who looks like that? Praise God and sonny Jesus.*

I cleared my throat. "Where did you say you're from, Ronald?"

"Souderton, Pennsylvania. Went to CD," he said, grudgingly returning his attention to me. "And I go by Hat, by the way. I got redcarded for what I did to the last guy who called me Ronald."

I nodded as if I understood what he meant.

"CD?" Autumn asked. She folded her arms across her breasts, presumably to keep them out of Hat's view. She still hadn't sat down.

"Christopher Dock High School," Elise supplied.

"How many Mennonite high schools are there anyway?" Autumn asked her, pointedly ignoring Hat.

Elise shrugged.

"Counting New Canaan, nine in the United States, three or four in Canada," I said. "Are you from CD too, Elise?"

"Nah, I'm from Lancaster," she said absently, her large, dark-rimmed eyes flicking between Hat and Autumn. "I graduated from LMH last Sunday."

"Sounds nice," Autumn said.

Elise gave an uncomfortable laugh like a little snort. "We got new field hockey uniforms this year, but that's about as close as we get to 'nice.' Lancaster can be pretty dull. What about yous?"

"Both of us are from New Canaan," I said. "Talk about dull—the biggest event in our town is the parade of antique tractors and fire engines down Main Street every fall."

Elise snorted again.

"You're from Iowa?" asked Hat. "Hey yeah, we played you guys in soccer my freshmen year. Pounded the everloving balls out of you, seven-one. That must be why I recognize you," he said to Autumn. "Weren't you a cheerleader or something?"

"New Canaan doesn't have cheerleaders," Autumn said. "And I went to public school until my last semester."

"That's weird," Hat said, leaning forward earnestly. "You look so familiar."

"Sorry to disappoint," she said tightly. She finally sat down beside me.

I wanted to elbow Hat in the ribs and tell him to knock it off, that his version of charm would seem hammy in an Adam Sandler movie, but he seemed to get the hint on his own.

"So what's your story?" he asked me. "And what's the deal with the gloves? No offense, but you don't look like a weightlifter."

Autumn muttered something under her breath that almost certainly contained the word "cock."

"Arthritis," I said quickly. "Have you heard the urban legend about that kid who played so much Atari that he developed arthritis?"

Hat and Elise shook their heads in unison. "Atari?" Hat asked, a disbelieving smile growing on his face.

"Well, my console of choice was the Gamicon. But the principle's the same."

"That's horrible," Elise said softly. She wrung her hands unconsciously, as people often seemed to do when I told them about my arthritis.

"You get used to it," I lied.

Frau Werner appeared at the door again. "Autumn and Elise? Herr Schmidt is waiting in my office to discuss your service assignments."

4

Autumn and Elise stood and filed out of the room. As soon as the click of Frau Werner's heels had faded down the hall Hat moved to the seat beside me. "Damn, dude, I thought all Iowa girls were corn fed hogs."

"What?"

Hat casually swung an arm up and smacked my chest. "Oh come on. Your girl Autumn. Hotness. Kaboom."

"She's really pretty," I agreed uncomfortably.

"At first I thought I'd be stuck with that skinny rat-faced girl from Lancaster."

"Elise?"

Hat grimaced. "There's a reason we call Lancaster 'Skankaster.' But your pal—" he broke off suddenly. "You guys aren't dating or anything, are you?"

I shook my head, hoping that whatever was happening would end soon.

"Yeah, I didn't think so but I wanted to make sure. Bros before hos, right? I just wish I could figure out why she looked so familiar. Maybe we went to the same summer camp in middle school or something."

"Maybe," I said. "So do you already have a service assignment for the summer?"

Hat stood and meandered over to the cake table. "Foosball," he said, probably meaning *Fußball,* the German word for soccer. "I was team captain at CD. And now that American soccer is getting more cred with European teams I guess they want us to come train their kids to play."

"I thought American teams were a joke in Europe. At least that's what the soccer players at my school always said," I added quickly. Hat was glowering at me over his shoulder.

"David Beckham, Lothar Matthäus, and Thierry Henry all chose to play for American teams," he said as if this fact barred any further argument.

"So you're coaching then?"

Hat shrugged, speared a wedge of cheesecake with a fork, and shook it onto his plate. "Probably not Varsity. They'd have to pay me for that. But JV is a good possibility. My goal is to get those JV players beating the Varsity by the end of the summer."

"Do German teams have JV and Varsity?"

Hat turned again and frowned. "No offense, man, but you ask more retarded questions than my grandma and she's had Alzheimer's since I was born. Why wouldn't they have JV and Varsity? Soccer's huge over here. It's not like all the kids could play on one team. There's only eleven players on the field. The coaches would be calling in subs like every two minutes."

"Makes sense," I said doubtfully.

There was a loud hiss as Hat unscrewed the cap from a bottle of Mezzo Mix. "I'm sure some things will be different here than back home," he allowed. "Like, I bet German Adidas cleats are different than the ones at home. Just like they have BMWs over here that you can't get in the US. So I'll definitely have to buy some new shoes before I start coaching."

"Cool."

"Yeah," he agreed. "You want a drink or something? I bet it's pretty hard to open a soda bottle with those gloves on."

I wasn't thirsty but I was so surprised by this sudden display of kindness that I nodded. Hat opened a second bottle of Mezzo Mix and brought it over.

"Thanks."

He sat down again. "What about your service job? I'm guessing you won't be teaching anyone to play baseball. No offense."

"Something with history I hope." I thought of the castle Autumn had pointed out on the way here. "Like archiving or working in a museum somewhere. I'm hoping my German will be good enough to do something like that."

"History?" Hat said around a mouthful of cheesecake. "And you got arthritis from playing too many video games? No offense bro, but I think there might be a reason you and that Autumn girl are just friends."

I considered telling Hat that for someone who said "no offense" so often he made a truckload of offensive comments. Instead I took a sip of Mezzo Mix. It tasted like a cocktail of Coke and orange Kool-Aid.

"Don't get me wrong, I'm sure you're smart," Hat went on. "And I might have arthritis myself if I were in your position. But it sure as hell wouldn't be from playing video games."

Now it was my turn to frown at him.

"Oh come on. Autumn? If I had her to look at all the time I'd probably beat off until my hands—"

His eyes abruptly lost focus and his features smoothed in recognition.

"What?" I said after a moment, knowing full well I didn't want to hear what.

"I know where I've seen her before!" he practically yelled. "New Canaan doesn't have cheerleaders, my ass. They've got at least one and I paid ten bucks for the picture that proves it."

Voices were approaching our room from down the hallway again. "You know, I think—"

"Dude, you're friends with the Different Seasons girl?" Hat asked with more than a touch of admiration. "Maybe you're not such a douche after all."

I waited for him to say "no offense," but he wasn't even looking at me anymore. He stood up as Elise and Autumn came into the room. Autumn seemed to understand at once what had happened. Her eyes narrowed and swung down to me, pinning me to my seat. *I didn't do it,* I wanted to say. Nothing came out. I chugged my Mezzo Mix, wishing I could crawl inside the bottle once it was empty.

"I bought all four of your pictures," Hat told Autumn earnestly. He jammed his hands in his pockets as if trying to look relaxed.

"Thanks," Autumn said coolly. "Leon, Frau Werner said you're next. Her office is down the hall."

I tried to think of something to say to Autumn, some way to explain that I had tried to keep Hat talking about anything but her. And I continued trying to think of something to say all the way down the dark, cold hallway to Frau Werner's office. I was only distracted when I heard Frau Werner's mellow voice behind a partially closed door. When I didn't hear another person I understood that she must be on the telephone. After a few sentences I realized she was talking about me.

"*Seine Hände...*" she said in the same wistful tone my mother sometimes used when talking about my arthritis.

I stopped with my hand on the doorknob, Autumn and Hat suddenly as far from my mind as New Canaan was from St. Goar, and listened.

"*Er könnte vielleicht mit der Schreibmachine schreiben,*" she said doubtfully. "*Nein, nichts schwieriges...*"

I listened with growing frustration. I had always done extremely well on German tests, so why was I having such a hard time understanding her? I was pretty sure Frau Werner had mentioned something about me working on a typewriter, which might be a problem; I'd gotten decent grades in Freshman Keyboarding but of course that had been before the arthritis. Just the thought of splaying my fingers out over a keyboard sent a dull throb through my knuckles.

"*Er kommt,*" Frau Werner said with finality. "*Ja, ich erzähle es ihm. Ja. Tschüss.*" The telephone clicked in its cradle. "You may come in, Leon."

I slid guiltily into the office but she didn't appear upset that I'd been eavesdropping. She gestured for me to sit in one of the padded chairs in front of her desk. I did so, nearly kicking over a large potted plant on the floor beside her desk.

The whole office seemed to be buried in clutter—file folders stacked on every surface, books stuffed onto floor-to-ceiling shelves on both walls, a heavy wooden desk like an underground bunker covered in paper rather than earth. But the more I studied the office the more I detected an underlying organization. The folders were neatly stacked, all facing the same direction within their piles; the books appeared to be organized by topics that had been typed on labels stuck to every shelf. Even the desk, though mostly covered, had an open workspace in the center.

I thought of my dad's office at church, sparse and maniacally utilitarian without so much as a quilted wall hanging for decoration, and his notion that a person's office was a window into their brain. If so, I thought Frau Werner's brain must be crammed almost to bursting and fiercely compartmentalized.

"The condition of your hands is making a service placement difficult," she said without preamble.

"I'm sorry," I said automatically. I had expected her to hem and haw, to make polite excuses that still boiled down to the idea that no one in St. Goar wanted to babysit a crippled American teenager for the summer. I couldn't remember anyone in the last two years speaking so directly about my arthritis, not even my doctor. Frau Werner raised her eyebrows. "Sorry for what? You have far less control in the matter than I do." She slid her index finger down a pile of folders, drew one out, and flipped it open. "Your application says you are interested in history and the German language."

I nodded but a slow, queasy roil had begun in my stomach. This was it. Frau Werner was about to instruct me to pack up my backpack, zip up its special zippers, and get on home where I would be a burden only to my family. I hoped I would be able to make it out of her office without vomiting Mezzo Mix into her potted plant.

"How much of my telephone conversation did you understand a moment ago?" she asked.

I swallowed against a hard lump in my throat. "I didn't mean to listen," I said desperately. "All I heard was something about a typewriter and that you'd explain something to me. I just caught the very end of what you were saying."

"You understood that I was discussing your service assignment? I was speaking quietly and rather quickly. Plus you could not see my lips moving, nor hear the other side of the conversation." She sat back and studied me over steepled fingertips. "That is impressive."

I shrugged, not quite daring to believe my ears. Would she waste time complimenting my German if she was just going to ship me back to the States?

"*Übrigens,*" she said, "*wie finden Sie Sankt Goar?*"

"*Ganz schön,*" I practically gushed.

She wanted to know whether I liked St. Goar? Well, I told her that as far as I was concerned it was probably the most beautiful city in all of Germany. No, in all of Europe! I would be happy to do just about anything if she would let me stay here for the summer.

I could translate children's books for the local elementary school. I could write English versions of the tourist brochures for the castle museum up at Burg Rheinfels. Shoot, I could make English menus for the various ice cream shops and Turkish *Döner Kebab* stands Autumn and I had seen as we'd disembarked from the ferry yesterday afternoon.

Frau Werner was smiling. "Your German is very good, Leon," she said, switching back into English. "That should help in finding a service assignment. I am sorry I have not found one for you already. You must understand that your situation is unusual."

"Yes," I said earnestly. "Believe me, I understand that."

She stood abruptly. "Very good. I can see you are a resilient and talented young man. With luck I will be able to inform you or your host parents about an assignment by the end of the day."

I stood as well. "*Vielen, vielen Dank, Frau Werner.*"

She reached out to shake my hand but immediately thought better of it and dropped her hand back to her side. "Would you please send Ronald to my office next?"

My relief vanished instantly in a wave of dread. Hat and Autumn had been in the cake room together unsupervised for almost ten minutes. I imagined Autumn brandishing a broken soda bottle in Hat's face.

"I'll send him right away," I promised. "Thanks again."

I almost expected to hear shouting when I stepped out of the office but the hallway was blessedly silent. I didn't realize just how silent until I came to the door of the cake room and still heard no voices.

Uh-oh.

I took a breath and strode inside. Autumn had taken the chair just inside the door. Hat slouched listlessly beside her, a plate of cake crumbs on his lap. Elise faced away from the door, apparently perusing the cake table. I doubted this was the sort of "mixer" Frau Werner had intended.

Hat looked up when I stepped through the door. "My turn?"

"Yeah."

He shot an acidic glare at Autumn. "Too bad. As much as I love being ignored by an icy slut…"

"And as much as I love being hit on by an arrogant prick who can bench press twice his IQ…" Autumn countered sweetly.

Hat rose, red faced. "You know what? You're worse than a whore. At least a whore puts out when you give her money."

"If it's too hard to hold up my pictures with one hand, you could always pin them on the ceiling or tape them to your blow-up doll. Be creative."

"I'm outta here," Hat growled. He glanced at me on his way out the door. "Dude, you can keep your friend. Crazy bitch."

Autumn settled back in her chair, smirking. "Another satisfied customer."

5

No one spoke after Hat left. Autumn slumped in her chair and glared at the floor. Elise continued to hover at the cake table, shoulders hunched almost up to her ears as if tensed for a blow to fall across her back. I walked over to the table and tried to cut myself a piece of cheesecake. After two failed attempts I set the knife down.

"Don't want any?" Elise asked softly. Her already large eyes seemed to take up the whole middle third of her face. She looked like one of those moist-eyed girls in a Japanese cartoon. "I could help if you like."

I stared down at the table and felt my cheeks growing hot. Not only had Autumn offered to dress me this morning, Hat had also poured me a drink, and now Elise was getting me food. Forget Frau Werner finding me a service assignment—I could be the service assignment for the rest of the group.

"What does it feel like?" Elise asked.

"Arthritis?" I asked, surprised. From the corner of my eye I saw that Autumn was watching us.

Elise blushed and turned away, looking more than ever like an anime character. "I'm sorry."

"My dad says no one should ever be sorry for asking questions. Let's sit first though."

Elise glanced over at Autumn, timid as a chipmunk in bobcat country as Grandpa Martin might say, but she followed me over and sat down.

"Okay, you know the sound that really cold, dry snow makes when you walk on it? Like, kind of a squealing sound?" Elise nodded. Autumn did too. "If you could turn that sound into a physical sensation, sprinkle it with some big chunks of the rock-salt they dump on the highway to melt snow, and cram it all into your knuckles you'd be getting pretty close what my hands feel like most of the time."

"Why don't you take anything for it?" asked Autumn. "Aspirin or something."

"My parents don't believe in better life through chemistry. Dr. Elmore did say I could take a couple aspirin or Tylenol every morning when the pain is the worst but honestly it doesn't help much. If I wear my gloves all night the next morning usually isn't so bad. Last night was just...you know."

"Is that when you hurt your head?" Elise asked. "What happened, anyway?"

I started spinning a lie in my brain. I wasn't very good at it but I also wasn't about to disturb the uneasy peace forming peace between Autumn and Elise. I needed a simple story that would satisfy any questions that might arise once the bandage came off and revealed the line of stitches running from the center of my forehead to the bridge of my nose. What if I had snuck down to Klaus and Great's kitchen in the middle of the night, fell face first into the knife block in the dark and knocked one of the knives out of the block...

Autumn laid a reassuring hand on my thigh. "Leon stepped

between me and this big bear of a guy in a bar last night. The guy hit him with a broken beer bottle. I have a feeling he meant to hit me instead."

For a moment I thought Elise was going to spring up and flee to the cake table again but then a disbelieving smile began to flicker on her lips. "You mean you really were in a bar fight?"

I felt a goofy grin spread across my face, though for the life of me I didn't know why. "I guess so."

"Hat would be so jealous," Elise said.

Autumn uttered a startled laugh that was somewhere between a chirp and a snort, which evoked a ludicrously high pitched giggle from Elise. I thought the three of us might have just become friends.

Heavy, clacking footsteps in the hallway announced the return of Frau Werner. Hat was not with her. "The last student in our group will not be arriving until tomorrow and I will need to pick him up in Köln. Autumn and Elise, your service assignment at the greenhouse begins tomorrow morning, yes?"

The girls nodded.

"Leon, I will notify the Holzes when I have found an assignment for you."

"Thank you," I said, wondering if the mixer would start now.

"Thank you all for coming to the party," said Frau Werner dispiritedly. On her way out of the room she tossed a rueful glance back at the cake table and muttered, "*Ich kaufe immer zu viel Kuchen.*"

Elise and I quickly looked away from each other to keep from laughing. The three of us left the church together. We'd been there less than an hour but the gloom inside had left me strangely exhausted.

"That was some party, huh?" said Elise, stretching hugely. "I thought Frau Werner was about to start crying when she saw all that leftover cake."

The sun hovered almost directly above the town even though it was still only midmorning. Clear blue sky stretched over the valley, deep and inviting. A warm breeze carried the faintly green smell of the river through the street.

Autumn yawned as we started down the sidewalk. "What time is it back home?"

Elise laid the back of her hand against her mouth to stifle a yawn of her own. "Four in the morning in Pennsylvania. Three in Iowa."

Autumn groaned. "Oh my G—goodness," she finished, tipping me a wink. "I could sleep for a week."

"I read that the best cure for jetlag is exercise," I said. "You still want to have a wander around town? Elise, you could come too."

"Shouldn't you take a nap or something, Leon?" Autumn asked. "You and Klaus got back from the hospital super late."

"I can't sleep when it's light out," I said. "Never have been able to."

Autumn considered for a moment. "Okay, I'm in for a walk. Elise?"

Elise shook her head. "I sleep just fine during the day. Like Frau Werner said, I got here a couple hours ago and I barely even met my host family. I'll go sit with them for a few minutes and then take a nap."

"See you tomorrow at the greenhouse?"

"Bright and early," Elise promised.

We made our goodbyes at the main sidewalk where Elise turned left and Autumn and I turned right. Autumn dug out her guidebook and opened it up to the few pages dedicated to St. Goar. She read as we walked. "Looks like we have a couple museums to choose from. There's also the big castle on the hill—that's a little more expensive than the museums…hmm. Oh, here we go. Somewhere around here there's a big rock called the Lorelei. It's supposedly shaped like a naked woman. Any of this grabbing you?"

I shrugged. "What if we just walk around this morning? Check out the town, take pictures of the *Fachwerkhäuser*."

"I thought you didn't like when people swore," Autumn said.

"*Fachwerk* is the triangular brown and white trim on all these houses. It's a big deal in Germany."

She rolled her eyes. "I'm just screwing with you, Leon. I do remember a few things from German class. Mrs. Miller talked about *Fachwerk* like every day."

"Sorry."

"If we're going to be friends, you have to relax around me."

"Sorry."

She grabbed my upper arm and pulled me to a stop. I thought she was going to yell at me but her attention was back on the guidebook. "Can you help me with this map?"

We leaned over the book together. A few wisps of her hair brushed my cheek in the breeze. The map was handdrawn and dotted with little symbols: crosses to signify churches, forks for restaurants, beds for motels, an H with a circle around it for the hospital, and so on. I noticed the Mennonite church wasn't labeled.

"We're here." I pointed to the left side of the map. "See? The town runs from north to south along the river."

"So the street we're on now just empties into a huge field," she said, squinting. "That's weird, it looks like there's an old church out in the middle of it."

I looked up from the book. Tall, narrow homes on both sides of the curving street hid whatever lay beyond them. "We can go look if you want. That map isn't very detailed. The empty part could be land owned by the government, empty grassland, vineyards, minefields…"

"Minefields?" she asked, startled.

"Just screwing with you," I said.

As we looked at each other, our faces only inches apart, some unidentifiable emotion flashed across her features. Whatever it was quickly disappeared behind a smile. She punched my arm softly. "Jerk."

"Well, if there is a church out there, we should go check it out. I'm under strict orders from my parents to take a picture of every old church I come across this summer. We could eat our lunches out in the field too. Like a picnic or something."

She was still smiling. "It's a date."

6

Autumn and I ate our sandwiches on the south face of a high grassy hill overlooking a wide plain. As Autumn's book had promised, a church did indeed sit about a hundred yards away from us. It looked like it hadn't served as a sanctuary to anything but birds and wildflowers for decades. Where three of the church's outer walls had once stood, piles of stones and mortar reared up from thick patches of tall yellow grass like trees in a haunted forest. The long south wall of the nave was still standing, complete with the flying buttresses that had held it up for who knew how many hundred years already but its central spire had collapsed at some point. Much of the stone was covered in faded soot from a long-ago fire. Capping the overall uninviting vibe of the place was a low barbed wire fence that ran haphazardly across the field between us and the abbey.

Autumn read aloud from her guidebook between bites of sandwich. "'The Abbey of Saint Anthony is the only building in St. Goar that is as old as Rheinfels Castle. It was bombed in 1944 because the Allies mistakenly believed the Germans were using it to store ammunition. Instead, several villages on the Rhine had collected their citizens' valuable art and stored it in the abbey for safekeeping, much in the same way the nearby Cologne Cathedral had been filled with priceless paintings, sculptures, tapestries, and ceramic artwork by Germany's most famous artists. The Cologne Cathedral and the art inside it survived the war, unlike the abbey.'

"Pricks," she whispered.

We finished our sandwiches in silence, watching traffic on the river. Massive cargo tankers lumbered downriver alongside tiny private motorboats and passenger ferries like the one Autumn and I had ridden from Cologne to St. Goar. If not for the frothy wakes behind the boats, the river would have looked as smooth and calm as brown plate glass.

Oddly enough, I was having trouble paying attention to the view of the river, which I guessed would be staggering even for someone who hadn't grown up in central Iowa. Whether due to my conversation with Hat or the hyperbolically romantic setting I found I couldn't take my eyes off of Autumn. Hat had used the words "hotness" and "kaboom" to describe her, and while these adjectives were crude I couldn't argue. But she was more than those things, too. With strands of shining blond hair whipping around her smooth cheek and graceful neck she wasn't anything so basic as hot.

The warm breeze strenghthened briefly into a gale that whipped across the hill and the low neckline of Autumn's tanktop whipped right along with it. I kept telling myself I was being a creep but the part of my brain that controlled my eyes refused to look away. Creamy white tanlines curved along the inner edges of her bra.

At last I glanced up guiltily, terrified I'd be caught staring. In her single semester at New Canaan Autumn had earned a reputation for gliding through the halls like a Greek goddess on a hunt— beautiful, untouchable, and dangerous.

I also heard my mother's voice in my head, reminding me that girls like Autumn Springer only knew one way to interact with boys. Did she realize what her shirt was doing? Did she think that was the only way I would pay attention to her?

But such thoughts were unfair. Without the forbidding, hard edges around her eyes and mouth she wasn't Autumn Springer: Hottest Mean Girl in School or Autumn Springer: Internet Prostitute. She was just another outcast of New Canaan Mennonite High School.

I dragged my eyes to the field spread below us, to the burned abbey and the river beyond. "I feel like I should tell you your shirt is hanging open. I didn't mean to look," I added lamely.

Without taking her eyes from the countryside she casually reached up and slid the thin straps of her tank top upward, resettling the neckline just below her collarbone. "I'm sorry I got in that stupid fight with Hat," she said. "You can blame me if you never become friends."

I laughed in surprise. "I think that ship sailed before Hat and I even met. I'm not the sort of person he'd ever hang out with."

Autumn ripped a clump of grass out of the ground and pitched it fitfully into the wind. The blades scattered and swept down the hill. I tried to wrap my hand around another patch of grass but it merely slid through my glove.

"Doesn't it bother you?" Autumn demanded abruptly. "That because you don't play a sport or brag about all the girls you've nailed, guys like him won't ever really accept you?"

"'What you think of me is none of my business,'" I recited.

She whirled around, her expression startled and hurt.

"I don't mean you personally," I explained quickly. "It's a little mantra my mom heard from her Unitarian friend. It just means that people either will or won't like me and the only thing I can control is how much of my true self I reveal to them. My dad said it was New Age hogwash but I like it. 'What you think of me is none of my business.' Made high school easier for me, that's for sure."

Autumn shook her head in wonder. "You could have been a very good person for me to hang out with last semester. Maybe I wouldn't have been so great for you..."

I shrugged uncomfortably. My mother would agree with her. Then, again, Mom also agreed with her Unitarian friend about not caring what others think.

"You're fine so far," I said, hearing but not understanding the defiance in my voice.

She snorted humorlessly. "Yeah, I guess you don't have *that* many stitches in your forehead."

Another gust of wind ripped past us and sailed across the field on rolling waves of grass. I stuffed the plastic lunch bags deep into Autumn's backpack so they wouldn't blow away.

"Can I ask you a personal question?" I said.

"Go for it."

"Why did you come to Germany? I mean, I'm glad you did. I just—"

"Calm down, Leon. I've already asked myself that question several times. I remember almost no German from class, I never studied German history or culture. And I probably could have persuaded Jerry to give me an internship at the law firm this summer, which would look great on a résumé..."

"That's another question," I interrupted. "Why do you call your dad Jerry? He's your actual dad, right? Not your stepfather?"

"Actual dad," she confirmed. "You're looking at the only child of Shawna and Jerome Springer. I guess I just do it to piss him off. I mean, the guy named me Autumn Springer for crying out loud. I suppose I'm lucky my middle name isn't Summer. So if I have to go through life as Autumn Springer he can be Jerry Springer. It's childish, I know."

I didn't say anything.

Her bravado faded. "Actually this trip started out as Jerry's idea. He totally flipped when he found out about Different Seasons. My website."

I nodded uncomfortably.

"I thought I'd been so careful about it. I didn't start the website until after I turned eighteen so I was legally an adult. I had my own bank account and everything. Mostly I didn't expect it to be so successful. I mean, I sent out over four thousand eight-by-tens between Halloween and Thanksgiving break, when Jerry found out. At ten bucks a pop the money adds up real quick."

My eyes bugged. Forty thousand dollars in a few weeks? That was almost five times the money I'd earned in a year of fundraising for this trip and working part time at the church.

And then the rest of what she'd said caught up to me. "Wait, how can the Germany trip have been your dad's idea after he found out about your website? The money and stuff was due at the beginning of November."

"I had to pay extra," Autumn said, shrugging. "My late application is almost certainly the reason I'm with Elise for my service assignment instead of on my own. I hope she's not upset about getting a partner."

I would've been upset but I didn't say so. Although, I realized dully, having to share a service assignment would be miles better than not having one at all.

"So," Autumn went on, "one Friday Jerry came home from the mechanic in Iowa City just steaming mad. I didn't think much of it—he's always mad when he comes back from the mechanic because it reminds him that Mom got the Mercedes in the divorce and he drives a Dodge Stratus. But the real problem turned out to be that he'd spotted one of my pictures hanging on the bulletin board in the mechanic's office. It must've been the cheerleader pose because he mentioned seeing the ruby earrings Grandma left me when she died. I told him that he must've been looking really closely if he'd noticed my earrings." She sighed. "The conversation went downhill from there."

"Wow," I said stupidly.

"I knew I shouldn't have sent any pictures out locally but the money was rolling in and I didn't recognize any names."

"Didn't Mr. Bontrager at the post office ever wonder what you were doing?"

She shook her head. "I printed out postage and labels myself and dropped them in a bunch of different mailboxes."

"But who developed the pictures? It seems like someone in New Canaan must've known something," I insisted. "It's New Canaan."

Autumn cocked an eyebrow. "Leon, I'm not an idiot. No one helped me do this. Well, not unless you count Jerry's buying spree after Mom left. He got me a new digital camera, laptop, cell phone, color laser printer, MP3 player, luggage, shoes, clothes. His excuse was that I would need all of it for college. A side effect of this was that I suddenly had a more advanced photography studio than anything the public high school could offer. I opened my own credit card account the day I turned eighteen, and off I went."

"Wow," I said again. "You sure thought this all through."

Autumn seemed suddenly uncomfortable. "It wasn't like I had grand plans to get my boobs out and sell signed eight-by-tens to internet dirtbags. But when a cell phone picture of a freshman girl flashing at a party made the rounds at my old school I heard a couple guys offering someone five bucks to forward the picture to them. I thought, my God, men are such morons. They could pay for my college."

I let this idea sink in for a minute. "But why did so many of them buy prints if the pictures were on your site already?"

"Because my site was about what you couldn't see. I put up a couple photos of myself in regular clothes, shirt unbuttoned, leaning over a little, whatever." She reddened. "You could only see segments of the actual pictures for sale. A crease of skin, a swell of breast, a loose bikini strap. Just enough to imply that if they bought the prints, they'd see a whole lot more than what was visible in the pictures on the site. It's the same concept behind burlesque."

Those curved tanlines swam into my mind. I pushed the image away. "Didn't any of your customers try to put the pictures they bought online so other people could see them for free?"

"Sure," Autumn said easily. "But my pictures are copyrighted. Every night I did some searching online. Whenever I found my pictures I pretended to be a lawyer and threatened the hosting site with legal action. I've worked enough summers in my dad's office to know some basic legal terms and phrases. Piece of cake."

I might have argued that nothing Autumn had just described sounded like a piece of cake but just then movement down in the ruined abbey caught my attention. A figure had just emerged from the abbey's cracked and leaning central door frame. Something about the person's stance and overall slimness made me think it was a young girl. Black hair blew around her face and bare shoulders.

Autumn still hadn't seen the girl. "Are you just going to ignore me now?" she demanded, twisting around to face me. Her irritation vanished when she saw my expression and she followed my line of sight down to the abbey. "Whoa, is that a person down there? Is she trying to kill herself? The whole place looks like it could crumble any second."

We watched the girl in silence for a few moments. Even from this far away it was plain she was moving slowly and carefully. But apparently she wasn't careful enough. She stumbled down the last of the abbey's wide front steps and collapsed into the tall yellow grass.

7

Autumn and I sat in shocked silence. My heart seemed to have stopped, perhaps waiting for the girl to stand up again before starting to beat again. The patch of grass where she had fallen swayed in the wind. The girl herself seemed to have disappeared completely. For one delirious second I was sure I'd imagined her but then I remembered Autumn had seen her too.

"Come on," I said, jumping to my feet and taking off down the hill.

The downslope of the hill was steeper than it appeared from the top. My hands throbbed with every slightly out of control step. Somehow I reached the foot of the hill without falling. Only the ancient, low-slung barbed wire fence now stood between me and the abbey. A metal warning sign swung on the fence, squalling on its rusty hinges. I saw the word *Achtung!* before I hurdled the wire.

My first thought as I came upon the girl in the grass was that she was dead. She lay on her side, knees hiked up halfway to her chest, one arm pinned awkwardly underneath her. From far away she had appeared slim. Up close she looked almost starved. Her one visible eye was half open and too deep in its socket. Whitish grit coated the fine hair around her temples.

I sank to my knees beside her, breath whistling like a boiling teapot, and laid a hand on her shoulder. Her eyelid fluttered weakly and her face rolled up slightly to look at me. Goosebumps flared up and down my arms. I fell backward in surprise.

Salvia?

"Who—" Autumn wheezed from behind me. "Who's Salvia?"

I looked around in surprise. Had I spoken aloud?

I turned back to the girl, who was making a feeble effort to lift her head off the ground. She was Salvia: the same high cheekbones and pointed chin; the same delicate mouth and almond shaped eyes; the same long hair, so black it almost looked blue.

But that was ridiculous. Worse than ridiculous, in fact. It was self-delusional and irresponsible and stupid. The girl from my favorite video game could not have just staggered out of a decrepit German abbey. Never mind that for three years Salvia had been more real to me than any of the girls at school or church.

"You know this person?" Autumn asked, starting to catch her breath.

"No," I said firmly.

Still on her side, the girl struggled to turn her face upward toward the sound of our voices. Autumn and I gasped together when we saw the left side of her face. A shiny purple bruise had swelled her left eye mostly shut, and the visible bit of eyeball showed a crimson web of broken blood vessels. Two half-healed pressure cuts bisected her left eyebrow and upper lip in perfectly straight black lines.

The wind swirled against the abbey's sagging walls in a miniature dust devil, slinging a painful storm of dirt and pebbles all over the place. The girl's eyes squeezed shut and she stirred as if trying to sit up.

"It's okay, sweetie," Autumn said, laying a hand on the girl's bare upper arm. "We're going to help you."

The girl's good eye flicked deliriously between Autumn and me. "*Wir möchten dir helfen,*" I attempted. "*Kannst du aufstehen?*" She didn't seem to understand German either.

"Son of a bitch," Autumn hissed. "Leon, who did this to her?"

I shook my head helplessly.

Autumn gathered herself. She held her hand out to the girl as one might do to a strange dog and spoke more softly. "It's okay. We just want to help."

Whatever language the girl spoke, she seemed to understand Autumn's gentle body language. With obvious effort, she lifted her arm and grasped Autumn's outstretched hand.

"Good," Autumn soothed. "Help me, Leon."

The girl tried to grab my hand as well. A deep ache rolled up my whole arm when her fingertip brushed my glove. I hooked my elbow under her armpit and hauled her up as gently as I could. Autumn and I each slung one of her arms across our shoulders and began walking over to the fence.

"She doesn't weigh a thing," Autumn said grimly. "I wonder how long she's been out here."

The girl's arm felt gritty against the back of my neck. Her hair had an earthy, stale odor to it.

"A few days?" I guessed.

The girl sporadically kicked along the ground as we walked. Her head lolled against my cheek then rose again. "*Chom towajushi su issushinayo?*" she mumbled. "*Chonun souleso salgo issum ni da.*"

"Don't worry, we're taking you to a doctor," Autumn told her. The girl slumped again and Autumn turned back to me. "What language was that?"

"Japanese," I said tightly. I didn't know what God was playing at by depositing this girl into my life but I would've been an idiot not to accept her for what she was: a living incarnation of a girl from a video game…and the only girl I'd ever loved.

"God, Leon, how many languages do you speak?"

I ignored her blasphemy. "I don't actually speak any Japanese but I heard enough of it back in my gaming days to know pretty much what it sounds like."

"So you don't know what she said," Autumn pressed.

"No idea," I admitted, trying not to sound annoyed. What did it matter if the girl was speaking Japanese or Swahili? What mattered was that she was hurt and we had to help her. Besides, I wouldn't have needed to hear a single word come out of her mouth to know she was Japanese. To know she was Salvia.

She's not Salvia! insisted the sane half of my mind savagely.

We reached the barbed wire fence. A quick study up and down its length revealed no gate or break in the wire. Loose, rusty snares of the stuff jutted out of gnarled fence posts and waved menacingly in the wind like the vines of some carnivorous plant. And this was not the regular sort of barbed wire you could find on a farm in Iowa. The barbs were an inch long, sharp and cruelly curved like dinosaur claws. I was lucky not to have impaled myself on one of them as I'd hurdled the fence.

"Take her a second," Autumn said. She carefully pulled the girl's arm from her shoulder and laid it across my other shoulder. I felt a little thrill as the girl locked her fingers behind my neck and laid her head against my chest. Autumn crept between two loose wires in the fence one leg at a time. Safely on the other side, she dusted her hands on the front of her shorts.

"Okay, I think I can keep her upright while you climb through and then maybe we can lift her over together."

I was barely listening. A single image from *Endless Saga*—the videogame I'd played so much and for so long that my hands had curled into useless claws before my sixteenth birthday—popped into my brain and wouldn't leave: Typhoon and Salvia on board the spaceship Naglfar after he'd saved her from a frigid death in the vacuum of space.

You came for me, Typhoon. I can never thank you enough.

You were in danger. I would have done the same for anyone.
Just hold me. Don't let go. I need to know I'm alive.

I tightened my hold on the girl's waist. "You're alive," I whispered, and before I could talk myself out of it I reached down and swept her up into my arms. Autumn had been right—the girl weighed almost nothing.

"Jeez, be careful!" Autumn warned.

But I wasn't going to drop the girl. I couldn't drop her. I didn't know how she'd gotten here or why but no one was going to hurt her again. Not if I had to stay with her in St. Goar forever.

I took two steps forward, leaned my upper body out over the barbed wire fence, and set the girl's feet gently on the ground with Autumn's help. Autumn held her while I climbed over myself.

"Well done," said Autumn. She sounded shaken. "What now?"

"We carry her to the hospital."

"Do you remember how to get there? You were pretty messed up last night."

"It's on the map in your guidebook," I grunted, taking most of the girl's weight again so Autumn could search her backpack.

She drew out the book, located the correct page, and studied the map. "It's on the other side of the main square in town. Doesn't look like more than a mile or so from here."

We each took one of the girl's arms again. She seemed to be more alert now than when we'd first found her but I suspected she'd topple over again if we let her go. We started across the field toward town.

8

The girl's feet scarcely touched the ground between the abbey and the hospital where I had received my stitches the night before. We purposely skirted the busy thoroughfares directly around the main town plaza, feeling that it would be prudent to avoid delays and difficult questions from curious German citizens or, worse, police officers we might run into. The latter worried me most. Something about the shuffling, half-conscious girl between us seemed to emanate trouble if not outright illegality.

Even so, several pedestrians asked whether we needed assistance, looking rather relieved when we said no, and more than one car slowed as it drove past us. The first time I turned down help Autumn glanced over at me but she seemed to understand my caution.

The girl grew progressively heavier as we walked so that by the time we reached the hospital she seemed to have gained fifty pounds. I was drenched in sweat and had a cramp like a twisting knife in my lower back. The attending nurse shot to her feet when we entered the small lobby where Klaus and I had come last night for my stitches. I didn't recognize her.

"*Was ist passiert?*" she demanded. Her wide eyes flicked back and forth between the bandages on my face and the semiconscious girl draped between Autumn and me. We must have looked like we'd just escaped a war zone.

I wheezed out a quick explanation in German that the blond girl and I were fine but the other one needed help as soon as possible. I said we'd found her in this condition near the Abbey of Saint Anthony outside of town. I couldn't tell how much the nurse understood but she knew an emergency when she saw one. A second nurse, this one younger and smaller with short, feathery hair like a boy's and a somehow furious economy to her movements, arrived quickly to help us carry the girl to a padded table in one of the examination rooms.

This new nurse, whose nametag declared her name to be Gabi, began squeezing the girl's arms and legs for broken bones and probing gingerly at the bruising around her eye, all the while interrogating me in German: Who was the girl? Was she a friend of ours? Where was she from? How could her family be reached? Where did we find her? Had she been unconscious the whole time? Did we remove anything from her person?

When we couldn't answer any of her questions the nurse switched to English and started over, to equally limited success. At last Nurse Gabi shooed us out of the examination room and latched the door behind us. The first nurse from the front desk ushered us back to a line of padded chairs in the lobby. We each chose a seat and collapsed.

Despite my protests that I was both fit and healthy the nurse leaned over me and inspected my bandages and the stitches under them. When she was satisfied that I required no immediate attention she straightened up and said, "Gabi will have more questions for you when she has finished with the patient."

We nodded our understanding and the nurse returned to her desk.

"I think everyone in this country speaks English better than I speak German," I mused quietly.

"Lucky for me," Autumn said. "So what do we do now? Call someone?"

"We need to stay here until we find out if she's okay. And answer Nurse Gabi's questions, remember?"

Autumn cocked her head and studied me with her too-smart green eyes. "You've got a real damsel in distress thing, don't you?"

"There's nothing more important than helping other people," I said a little testily. My hands were starting to hurt again. "I would have—"

"Done the same for anyone, I know," Autumn finished. She didn't sound convinced.

I chose not to respond. Of course I would have helped anyone in the same situation as the girl. Autumn of all people should know that.

"What did you call her back at the abbey?" Autumn asked. "Samantha?"

"Salvia," I corrected automatically, feeling a not entirely unpleasant flutter in my stomach. "But she's not Salvia. I made a mistake."

Something in my expression seemed to worry her. "Is Salvia someone from school? Do I know her?"

I hesitated. "It's sort of embarrassing."

"Leon, have you already forgotten what I told you today? Do you know what will come up for the rest of my life when you Google my name?"

"I thought you said you stopped people from putting up your pictures."

"Yeah, for a couple weeks. That was half a year ago. Those pictures will be attached to my name for the rest of my life. Could you honestly tell me anything more embarrassing about yourself than that?"

I took a deep breath. "Salvia is the girl from *Endless Saga.*"

"Is that like a movie or something?"

"No. It's a game, but …" I floundered for the right words. "What I mean is, *Endless Saga* is *the* videogame. The game I was obsessed with when I was younger, and the reason I have arthritis."

"Yeah, how did that even work?" Autumn said. "The video game thing. I know there are certain Mennonites who use horses and buggies instead of cars and don't buy TVs or whatever."

"Those are the Amish," I corrected, seizing on the excuse to delay talking about *Endless Saga*. Besides, my father received questions about Mennonites and technology a lot when he went to multidenominational conferences and I thought I knew where Autumn was going with her question. "They're a branch of Mennonites that broke away from the church a long time ago."

"But most of the students at New Canaan High School came from families like yours that use electricity and telephones and stuff."

"Probably all of them," I agreed. "Our branch of the Mennonites, which used to be called the Old Mennonites, broke with the General Conference back in—"

"I don't care about any of that," Autumn interrupted, though she sounded amused. "I'm just wondering how the son of a Mennonite pastor could be allowed to play hours and hours of video games instead of memorizing Bible verses."

"Well, I did that too," I said. "And you're right. My dad wasn't real thrilled with my hobby. He called it a 'waste of time and a slow poison to my sense of morality.'"

"Yikes. And I thought Jerry got on his high horse sometimes. So why—"

"My mother," I said with a sigh. Here was another part of my life I hadn't ever planned on sharing with Autumn or anyone else. "In middle school she bought me a Gamicon at a garage sale thinking that if I had a video game system then maybe other kids might want to come over and play with me. I wasn't…popular."

"And her plan didn't work." It wasn't a question. Autumn had been at New Canaan long enough to know I still didn't have friends.

"It bothered my mom more than me," I said truthfully. "I've always been a loner."

"It's their loss," Autumn said. "Those other kids. Screw em."

"Yeah," I said awkwardly. "So anyway, I may not have had any friends, but I did have a second-hand Gamicon and the game *Endless Saga*."

"That's the game with the Saliva girl."

I burst out laughing. "Salvia—Sal-vee-uh. Not 'saliva.'"

Autumn was grinning. "Sorry."

"But yeah. And I don't know how or why, but that girl we just carried across town is—" I swallowed. "She looks a lot like Salvia."

Autumn considered this. "Because she's Japanese?"

I bristled. "What, you think I'm racist or something? We'll find a picture on the internet if you don't believe me. Her hair, the shape of her eyes, her mouth—she's Salvia."

Her smile completely gone, Autumn now looked very worried indeed.

"I mean, she looks like Salvia," I corrected hastily. "Exactly like her."

Autumn seemed to decide the girl's appearance was a dangerous line of questioning and switched gears. "So you said this Salvia was the main character in your *Endless Saga* game?"

"Not the main character. The sort of…love interest, I guess."

A red hot flush spread from my cheeks all the way down the sides of my neck. I considered asking Autumn if her mother hadn't ever taught her it was impolite to stare. Instead I turned away and pretended to cough.

She wouldn't be put off. "Leon, did you have a crush on the girl in your video game?"

And there it was. If Autumn didn't end our brief friendship on the grounds that I was a total freak then she would laugh at me and I would end our friendship myself. The girl who sold naked pictures of herself on the internet had the temerity to judge me?

Her hands closed gently, unexpectedly around my glove. I faced her as defiantly as I could.

"You don't need to be embarrassed. Look, lots of guys have crushes on movie stars, right? To my way of thinking there's no difference between digitally smoothing out an actress's skin in a close-up shot and creating a 3D model of a woman in a video game. Either way, the image is someone's idea of the perfect woman. The only difference between movies and video games is that most people playing games can accept that the girl on the screen isn't real."

Before I could respond—or even figure out how to begin to respond—little Nurse Gabi pounded through the door into the waiting room, causing Autumn and me both to jump in our seats. She stopped a few feet away from us and announced, "*Die Patientin ist aufgewacht.*"

Autumn leaned over and asked in a nervous whisper, "What'd she say?"

I swallowed again. "She says the girl's awake."

9

Nurse Gabi led us past the front desk and through the short hallway to the examination room where we'd left the girl. She still lay on the room's adjustable bed, now wearing a white hospital gown, torso propped up by several pillows. The ragged clothes she'd been wearing earlier were folded neatly on a chair just inside the door. The girl herself had been restored to a higher sort of order as well. Her cheeks and forehead were clear of dirt smudges and now revealed a perfectly smooth, if ashen, complexion. A white plastic icepack obscured her bruised left eye. Two strips of medical tape had closed the cut on her upper lip. An IV tube ran from another patch of tape on the back of her left hand to a bag of clear fluid hanging on a metal stand beside her bed.

Her right eye widened uncertainly when the door opened but her expression cleared when she saw Autumn and me. She struggled to sit up. Nurse Gabi moved to her side at once, pressing her shoulders gently back against the bed. The girl gave up and looked hazily between Autumn and me. She bobbed her head once in what was obviously a truncated bow. "*Kam sa ham ni da,*" she said softly.

Autumn returned the head bob but muttered to me, "I thought thank you in Japanese was *arigato.*"

I shrugged. "I'm sure there are lots of ways to say it. You know, formal or informal like the German *Sie* and *du.*"

"The patient is from Japan?" Nurse Gabi asked.

"Japan," I confirmed. Autumn glanced at me but I ignored her.

"She had no identification when you discovered her?"

Autumn shook her head. "And she passed out before we could even try to figure out her name."

"Is there an official Japanese translator in St. Goar?" I asked.

Nurse Gabi smiled wryly. "I will be surprised if there is one in Köln. Perhaps another nearby city will have a Japanese Consulate and a translator. Otherwise the Japanese Embassy in Berlin will be our best option. They can also replace her passport if she has truly lost it. I will send them her photograph and the details about how she was found in St. Goar. They can contact our office if they have questions."

She moved over to a counter covered with jars and boxes of sterile medical equipment and picked up an ornate golden box about the size of a cigarette case. "Does either of you recognize this?"

The box appeared to be made of brass and was almost entirely covered in delicate carvings except for a square on the front where an intricate raised symbol had been either painted or dyed in bold red.

I stared hard at the symbol but I couldn't recognize written Japanese any better than the spoken language. It may have been the girl's name, a price tag, or an artistic flourish.

Next the nurse thumbed the clasp on the side of the box and swung the lid open. Inside was a collection of nasty looking needles of varying lengths and thicknesses. Each had a tiny cylindrical grip that was carved and painted as ornately as the box itself.

My heart froze in my chest. "Drugs?" I whispered.

Nurse Gabi shook her head. "These are not hypodermic needles. They could be used for purposes such as sewing, acupuncture, or even decoration. I simply wondered if the markings on the case or needles could be a family name or other identification."

"I'm sorry, I can't read Japanese," I said.

Nurse Gabi closed the little case carefully before returning it to the counter. "I cannot talk about the patient's injuries or the tests we performed with anyone but her family or the proper government officials. We—"

"Was she sexually assaulted?" Autumn asked quietly.

"What?" I asked, appalled. Had she noticed something that I hadn't?

Nurse Gabi frowned, watching Autumn carefully. "I cannot—"

"It's bad enough that she's hurt and alone without anyone she can talk to," Autumn said in that same quiet voice. "I couldn't stand it if she'd been raped too."

The furrow in Nurse Gabi's brow smoothed. "As I said, I cannot discuss the patient's injuries with you—"

Autumn made a disgusted *tch!* sound.

"—but…I suppose I can tell you what did not happen."

Autumn's eyes closed and she took a deep, shuddery breath before nodding. "Thank you."

"We will keep her in the hospital overnight," Nurse Gabi went on, now speaking to me, "but after that is there somewhere she can stay until the Embassy is able to replace her identification?"

"Do you know Anna Werner?" I asked, still rather shaken by Autumn's question. At least it seemed like the answer had been no. "She is the director of the program we're in. I'm sure she'll know of a place."

At the mention of the Frau Werner, Nurse Gabi looked down at my gloves as if noticing them for the first time. "You are the young man with arthritis. Frau Werner contacted us about you last month." She held out her hand. "I am called Gabi."

"Leon," I introduced myself. "Sorry, I don't shake hands."

"Ah. Naturally."

Autumn held out her own hand. "I'm Autumn Springer. Thanks for all of your help. Your English is wonderful, by the way."

Nurse Gabi grinned. It made her look even younger.

Autumn stretched her arms above her head and turned to me. "Now that we know she's okay I'll go home to tell Klaus and Greta what's happening. Besides, I think I'm ready for that nap after all."

"Can you find your way back if I stay here a little longer?"

She nodded and stifled a yawn with the back of her hand. "Thanks for your help, Gabi. It was very nice to meet you." The two of them shook hands once more and Autumn left the room.

"Has she eaten anything?" I asked Nurse Gabi, indicating the girl, whose good eye had closed again. "I think she's been living outside for a couple days."

Nurse Gabi glanced up from her notes. "I was going to give her some *Flädlesuppe*. If she responds well she can try more solid foods. It is dangerous to eat very heavy food after even short periods of starvation."

Mrs. Miller had treated the German 4 class to *Flädlesuppe* during our final exam last month. If I remembered correctly, the soup had consisted of soft German pancakes floating in a meat broth.

"I could help her eat if you've got other things to do," I said. "I'd like to stay with her until I know she's feeling better."

Nurse Gabi smiled again, this time a little sadly. "That is a good idea. I do not think many people have been nice to her lately."

She left the room to get the soup. I pulled a chair to the side of the girl's bed. "Hi," I said. "Um, *konnichiwa?*"

Her right eye opened and rolled toward me again, clearly surprised. "*Nihongo wo wakaru?*"

I smiled apologetically. "I only know like five Japanese words. Maybe you can teach me some of your language and I'll teach you some of mine."

I thought I saw the slimmest hint of a smile but other than that she did not respond. It was a start.

"My name is Leon." I placed my hands against my chest. "Lee-yon," I enunciated.

Her eye swung down to my hands, then back up to my face.

Suddenly I laughed. "Maybe if I just talk slower and louder you'll understand, right? Just like if I was in a Japanese hospital, all the doctor would have to do is slow down his speaking a bit and I'd understand every word. I'm an idiot."

I sighed. "I'd love to know your name too. I can't keep calling you 'the girl.'" I glanced back at the door and lowered my voice. "Your name's not Salvia, is it? I mean…you just look so much like her."

Her expression had softened but not in response to the name. She was looking at my hands again.

"*Mahlzeit,*" Nurse Gabi announced, breezing back into the room with a steaming bowl on a tray. "*Flädlesuppe für das hübsche Mädchen.*"

The girl instantly seemed to forget all about me. Her right eye fastened brightly on the bowl of soup. She struggled to sit up once more and this time Nurse Gabi did not try to stop her. The ice pack dropped into the girl's lap. Between her newly washed face and the room's fluorescent lighting, her bruise looked shiny and even more painful than before. She lifted the soup bowl in both hands and slurped greedily.

"She does not care that I forgot the spoon," Nurse Gabi said affectionately.

The broth disappeared in less than a minute. Next the girl pulled the long strips of pancake from the bowl between her slender forefinger and thumb and chewed them into her mouth inch by inch, her face dipped into the bowl in the same posture my dad adopted when he ate spaghetti. When she had finished she beamed at Nurse Gabi and bobbed her head once in thanks.

"*Bitte sehr,*" said Nurse Gabi, sounding as pleased as the girl looked. She took the empty bowl and set it back on the tray. "*Eine Stunde noch und Du bekommst mehr,*" she told the girl kindly.

She turned to me. "Would you like to stay with her a bit longer?"

"If it's okay."

"I must fill out the documents to send to the consulate. You will call me if she becomes ill from the food?"

I promised I would and Nurse Gabi left again. The girl had lain back and replaced the ice pack over her swollen left eye. Her right eye resettled on my hands as I struggled to drag a chair closer to her bed.

"They're hurting again," I explained, sitting down. "No point in moaning about it, though. Especially when you're in worse shape than I am. I wish you could tell me how you got here and who did this to you. And why you look so much like her."

She removed her hand from the icepack over her eye and reached for mine.

"Ah, no thank you. Letting someone touch my hands right now would be an extremely bad idea. Owie," I added pointlessly.

She didn't move, just held her hand out impassively as if she could wait all day.

I blew out a shaky breath. "Just be careful, okay?"

I laid my right hand into hers. She turned it over delicately, studying the fingertips, which had started to swell against the edges of the glove. She fingered the Velcro catch at the glove's base.

This was going from bad to worse.

She worked with both hands now, mindful of her IV, and gently pulled open the Velcro. My heart was racing and sweat was gathering at my temples.

"Getting the fingers out is the hardest bit," I told her, reaching over to help.

She shook her head firmly. When the icepack slid down into her lap again she didn't bother to pick it up. The added weight of the pack pulled the front of her gown tight against her breasts. A thought popped into my mind before I was able to push it away: *They're smaller than Autumn's.*

I turned my head forcefully away. What was wrong with me? First staring down Autumn's shirt like a creep, and now—

The girl suddenly jammed her fingers inside my glove and squeezed, pressing hard against two spots on my palm and one on the back of my hand.

"Hey!"

My hand jerked instinctively but she held on. After a few seconds I realized something altogether wonderful was happening. Slow, cool numbness was spreading through my knuckles from the three points where she was squeezing. The remaining pain felt deep and faraway, drowned in the liquid serenity radiating from her fingertips.

"How are you doing that?"

She didn't answer. With her fingers still pressed into those three spots on my hand, she used her other hand to slide the glove off. I barely felt it. She set the glove in her lap beside the ice pack and pointed at the counter across the room. I turned to look and saw the little gold box with the red symbols on it.

I cleared my throat. "You want your needles?"

"*Hae juseyo,*" she said in a tone that brooked no argument.

She let go of my hand and I retrieved the box, carrying it to her in an impossibly pain-free grip. She unfastened the catch on the side of the box with a practiced motion, laid the box in her lap, which was now becoming quite full, and reached out once more. I gave her my hand willingly this time. I hadn't cared much for needles before the arthritis, but I ached so badly all of the time now that the prick of a needle at the doctor's office seemed like a tickle in comparison.

She probed my swollen knuckles with that same unbelievably gentle touch and clucked her tongue once.

"That bad, huh?" I asked, attempting to smile.

In answer she turned the hand over and prodded several points, beginning at the wrist and moving up toward the fingers. I had decided she wasn't going to use her needles after all when she selected one from the little gold box and unceremoniously stabbed it into the back of my hand, near the wrist.

I jerked back even harder this time and she looked up reproachfully. "*Chamkan manyo,*" she chided.

"Sorry, I just—"

She took my hand once more and quickly inserted seven more needles into carefully chosen spots on the front and back of my hand. The twisting, writhing, molten pain that had been as tied to me as my own shadow for the past two years dissolved in a wash of ice and calm. I thought this must be how a polar bear feels when it slips into the freezing ocean for its first bath after a long, stale winter of hibernation.

"Ree-yong," she said, tugging gently on my arm. It took me a moment to realize that she was saying my name.

"Yes. I'm Leon. Leon Martin, that's right. And you're a gift from God."

"Shin Oon-myung," she said, pointing to herself and returning the goofy smile I felt on my own face.

"Shin," I said. "You have a beautiful name. Thank you, Shin. Thank you."

She bobbed her head one more time and reached for my other hand.

DISC 2

1

I woke up without my gloves on for the second day in a row. However, whereas yesterday I had felt like the world might end with the level of pain in my hands, today the sun outside my skylight seemed to be rising on a brand new life. Melodramatic? No. Two years of chronic pain had brought a desperation I couldn't have imagined before I'd lived with it, and even then it had been impossible to tell how the pain had affected every aspect of my life until it was gone.

I reached over to the travel alarm clock beside my bed. Even though my bedroom was bright enough to see the time I still pressed the little button that lit the display. Simply because I could.

I raised my hands to my face and studied their backs and palms, turning them over again and again. Tiny red dots hardly larger than the pores in my skin were all that remained of Shin's treatment yesterday. I set my palms together and laced my fingers between them, playing a game my old Sunday school teacher had taught us.

"Here is the church," I whispered.

I lifted my index fingers and set the tips together to form a triangle. "Here is the steeple. Open the doors…"

I turned over my intertwined hands to reveal a mess of wiggling fingers as I finished the old rhyme: "…and see all the people."

Thank you, God.

"Shin Oon-myung."

Goosebumps flared across my forearms. I felt like I was in first grade again, lying in bed and whispering the name of the girl I liked in school. I wondered if I should bury my face in a pillow and giggle just to complete the memory.

I sat up and located the shorts I'd worn yesterday amid a rumpled pile of clothes on the floor. Folded in the side pocket was half of the sheet of paper Nurse Gabi had provided Shin and me to write our names for each other (that I could write at all with a regular ballpoint pen was nothing short of miraculous, but yesterday had evidently been my day of miracles).

As I'd explained to Autumn, the Japanese language employed more than one alphabet, and Shin had first scrawled her name in three symbols that reminded me inexplicably of circuit boards inside a computer.

신 운명

The characters were lovely, but unfamiliar to the point of being alien. All I could tell was that each one must represent a syllable of her name. When it was plain that the letters meant nothing to me, Shin had tried again, writing much more ornate letters with long, deliberate strokes.

申運命

I didn't recognize these characters any better than the last, and I shrugged to show my lack of understanding. She squinted up at me, lips pursed in contemplation, then scratched a final series of symbols on the paper.

シンウンミュン

She wrote these with an air of careless haste, as if she didn't really expect me to understand them any better than the last. And they were indeed unintelligible to me but they seemed more familiar than the others somehow. Perhaps this third type of text was more common in Japanese video games than the first two.

All of a sudden I wished desperately for my old Gamicon. To hear the grave Latin choral music that introduced players to the world of *Endless Saga*. To see Salvia on my television screen, standing in a field of yellow grass with pink flower petals whipping around her in a tornadic spiral and washing her black hair upward on the breeze.

Except, I realized, I didn't need a television or a Gamicon to see Salvia again. The real Salvia was lying in a hospital bed just a few blocks away, possibly slurping down another bowl of *Flädlesuppe* at this very moment. And Nurse Gabi had suggested that she might be able to leave the hospital today.

For the first time since yesterday's meeting with Frau Werner I was glad she hadn't found me a service assignment. I leapt out of bed and pulled on my shorts and a t-shirt. The half sheet of paper with the different versions of Shin's name on it went back into my pocket—I'd forgotten how quick and easy the processes of dressing and paper-folding could be. I almost wished I had a pair of shoes with laces so I could try my hand at tying them after two years of using only Velcro.

I stopped in the bathroom to run a wet comb through my hair and headed downstairs. Klaus and Autumn were already sitting at the little kitchen table.

"Good morning!" Klaus bellowed.

Greta looked up from a pot of boiling eggs and beamed at me. *"Guten Morgen, mein Junge. Ach, dein Gesicht,"* she mourned.

The bruises around the inner areas of my eyes had deepened further overnight—I'd reminded myself of a rather harried looking raccoon in the bathroom mirror—but I assured Greta that my head didn't hurt as bad as it had yesterday.

Autumn's eyes flicked down to my hands as I dropped into the seat beside her. I had declined her help in putting on my gloves before bed last night, explaining what Shin had done with her needles.

"So the acupuncture really worked, huh?" Autumn asked now.

"It's unbelievable." I selected a hard roll from the basket of bread on the table. "I mean, I feel a little twist somewhere deep in there but it's like having a whole new pair of hands."

She smiled distractedly. "That's really great, Leon."

"I believe the Autumn is nervous for her first day of work, yes?" Klaus boomed happily. Greta clucked from the stove, obviously annoyed that Klaus still wasn't speaking German with us.

"The Autumn is just fine," Autumn said sweetly.

I doubted this very much but it seemed unwise to argue. "Are you meeting Elise at the church or the greenhouse?"

"The greenhouse. In fact I'd better get going." She wiped her mouth and stood. *"Frau Holz, danke for the Früh...* for the breakfast."

Frau Holz's expression said she wanted to cluck disapprovingly again at Autumn's clumsy mixture of German and English but she restrained herself and pecked Autumn's cheek. *"Viel Glück, Kind."*

Autumn touched my shoulder on her way out. "Have fun today. Don't get into any more trouble. At least not without me."

When she had gone, Klaus turned his tiny, cheerful eyes to me. "And what will you do today?"

"I'm going to the hospital."

"Ach so! Wann kommt das Mädchen nach Hause?" Greta asked, sounding a bit panicked.

I explained that Shin wouldn't be coming back to the Holz's house until later this afternoon. I thanked them both again for allowing Shin to stay here until her identity and documentation could be sorted out.

"*Kein Problem!*" Klaus said. "No problem, yes? What is the English expression? The more who are marrying..." he trailed off expectantly.

"The more the merrier," I corrected, which elicited nearly hysterical laughter from him. His eyes disappeared completely and his belly trembled.

I swallowed the last bite of a hard roll and pungent white cheese. "I'd better be going too."

Greta looked even more scandalized than usual. "*Du hast gar nichts gegessen.*"

I promised I would eat more at the next meal.

"In that case I will eat enough breakfast for both, yes?" Klaus suggested with a wink. Greta told him just what she thought of that idea and their subsequent argument allowed me to slip out the door without any more hassle.

2

Klaus and Greta's home sat, like all of the nearby homes, less than a block away from the river atop a manmade plateau aptly named Oberstraße—Overstreet. Their tiny front yard was bisected by a narrow sidewalk terminating in a stone staircase that led down to street level. I turned left on the sidewalk, the river to the right and the street's floodwall on my left.

After perhaps a quarter mile the street curved away from the river and widened into the town's central *Marktplatz,* a wide plaza of bakeries, pharmacies, shoe stores, and supermarkets. A small cathedral—two words I wouldn't have thought to put together until our taxi had driven past the monstrous gothic cathedral in Cologne two days ago, making all subsequent cathedrals seem small—dominated the western end of the square, its imposing iron doors standing open to welcome worshippers, tourists, and the cool morning air. The modest Deutsche Bahn train station on my left marked the southern edge of the town proper, beyond which lay rolling grassland and impossibly steep vineyards carved into the sides of hills.

Now that I didn't have to worry about the humidity assaulting my hands, I thought I could get used to living in a place like this.

I cut across the *Marktplatz* onto a long street blocked on either end by rows of thick, waist-high concrete pillars that blocked all non-pedestrian traffic. This part of town seemed to cater mostly to tourists, with gaudy shops boasting outdoor racks of postcards and prepaid international telephone cards, ceramic beer steins, and baked goods. The smell of the morning's fresh hard rolls and Berliners—sugar-dusted jelly donuts—drifted through the street like a golden fog. Maybe on the way home, Shin and I could stop somewhere for a second breakfast.

A fresh wave of goosebumps pebbled my forearms. "Get a grip," I muttered.

The now familiar St. Goar hospital came into view up ahead, equidistant from City Hall, a Kindergarten, and a dank staircase leading down into the only public restroom I'd seen in the entire town so far. As always, the brooding cliff of Rheinfels Castle dominated sky to the northwest, but at this time of day the morning sun cast it in a discordantly cheerful orange light.

The thought came again as I pulled open the hospital's main door: I could get used to this.

The nurse who had been stationed at the front desk yesterday greeted me with a smile and asked me to wait a moment for Nurse Gabi. I sat down and concentrated on making the butterflies in my stomach quit their stupid flapping. After a minute Nurse Gabi came barreling into the waiting area, hand held straight out in front of her, prepared either to shake hands or cut a stack of boards with a karate chop. I startled myself by actually shaking her hand. It barely hurt.

"Hi," I said.

"Hi," she returned. In her clipped voice, the greeting did indeed sound like something a person would shout as they chopped a stack of boards. "You are here to collect your friend."

"If she's ready to go."

Nurse Gabi turned on her heel and indicated with a nod that I should follow her back to the rooms. "The clothing she was wearing when she arrived yesterday was torn and soiled," Nurse Gabi said over her shoulder, "but we keep clean clothes in the hospital for circumstances like these."

"I'm sure Shin appreciated that."

Shin stuck her head out from the doorway of her room with a questioning smile on her face as we approached. The swelling had gone down around her left eye, but the purple and yellow bruises looked as painful as ever. The cuts on her lip and eyebrow sparkled with some kind of ointment.

However, apart from her injuries she looked infinitely more alive, more vital than she had yesterday. Her new clothes undoubtedly helped in this respect. She wore a pair of khaki capris and a soft pink t-shirt with blue lettering that made the same phrase Klaus had used this morning at breakfast: *Kein Problem.* No problem. A cheap pair of flip-flops revealed chipped and uneven toenails that had at one time been artfully painted.

"Gap-pi?" Shin asked. Then she saw me and her smile changed somehow. I couldn't tell if my presence had improved her day or made it worse.

"Ree-yong."

At least she remembered my name. "*Konnichiwa, Shin.*"

Her smile changed again. And I'd thought Autumn was hard to read…

Nurse Gabi explained to Shin, in German, that she was healthy enough to leave the hospital and I would be taking her to a new home. Gabi obviously realized that Shin didn't understand a word of what she was saying but she said it all the same. She spoke quietly and respectfully, ending her short presentation by telling Shin it had been nice to meet her and she hoped that she and Shin could be friends if they met again.

Shin listened patiently, bobbing her head each time Nurse Gabi finished a sentence. When it was clear Gabi had finished Shin bowed low from the waist. "*Ko mab sum ni da.*"

"*Bitte sehr, Süße,*" Nurse Gabi said, wrinkling her nose with pleasure.

I turned to Shin and spoke as Nurse Gabi had—slowly, but not as if to a child. "Klaus and Greta Holz are going to let you stay with them for a while. I'm staying with them and so is Autumn, the other girl you met yesterday. So, if you're ready to leave…" I glanced at Nurse Gabi, who nodded. "We can go."

Shin bowed once more to Nurse Gabi before following me into the main lobby, where she bowed to the attending nurse. She also seemed to consider bowing to an elderly couple sitting together in the waiting area but settled for bowing to me again when I held the outer door open for her.

Shin and I must have made quite the pair, strolling down the middle of the *Fußgängerzone*—the street where no cars were allowed—with our bandaged and bruised faces. She clearly shared my interest in the delightful smells drifting from the many bakeries along the street and when she pointed to a basket of golden soft pretzels under a bakery sneeze guard I bought two of them.

Once we were out on the street again Shin accepted her pretzel enthusiastically. "*Mani duseyo,*" she said with obvious relish and began tearing away tiny chunks of it with her fingertips.

"You like to eat, don't you?" I asked, wrenching a big bite from my own pretzel. "My dad says I shouldn't trust girls who don't eat, so between your appetite and what you did to my hands yesterday you're just about batting a thousand."

She grinned, holding her small, talented fingers over her mouth.

"Hold onto that good mood," I told her. "You might see some things today you don't like. We're going back to the abbey where Autumn and I found you. Maybe you can show me why you were there, or give me some clue about who beat you up. Then I can tell the police and make sure it doesn't happen again, okay?"

She seemed to understand that I had said something serious because her next bite of pretzel was more subdued. Her enthusiasm returned soon enough, however, and by the time we were walking back through the *Marktplatz* she was practically spinning around like a ballet dancer to make sure she didn't miss a single sight. This thirst for life, for new experiences, was heavily contagious. I wished I had Autumn's guidebook to give names to everything around us.

When Shin stopped twirling to gape up at the huge castle on the cliff I realized I at least knew one name: "That's Burg Rheinfels. It's even older than the abbey where we found you. We can go there sometime if you want. It's like a museum. I don't think we'll have time today, though. The abbey is way on the opposite side of town."

Shin surprised me by nodding, her good eye fixed solemnly on the castle.

The walk to the hill on the edge of town took a mere ten minutes—a much shorter and more pleasant journey without having to support Shin's weight the whole way. She did another of her spinning moves to take in the river, vineyards, and towns visible from the top of hill but stopped dead when she caught sight of the abbey below us.

"It's okay." I reached down to take her hand. She blinked in surprise and glanced down when my fingers curled around hers.

"It's okay." I gave her hand a little tug.

She began moving but she was no longer looking around at the scenery. Her head stayed low, her dark eyes on the ground.

I might have been able to figure out what was bothering her had I not been so focused on the fact that I was holding hands with a girl for the first time. My arthritis had begun before I'd hit puberty—well before I'd ever understood the draw of having a girl's fingers wrapped in mine.

I released her when we reached the barbed wire fence and pulled down on the top wire so she could climb over. Once we were both inside she mounted the steps to what would have the front door of the abbey—the crumbling archway where I had first seen her yesterday—and bowed stiffly.

"*Ko mab sum ni da.*"

It sounded like the same thing she'd said to Nurse Gabi when we'd left the hospital less than an hour ago. Suddenly I understood why she had become so quiet on our way down the hill toward the abbey.

"No, no, I didn't bring you back here just to abandon you. I only wanted to know where you came from before we found you. You must have walked from somewhere, right?"

She rose halfway out of the bow and watched me uncertainly.

"Oh man, how am I going to do this?" I stared around the abbey but inspiration failed to burst from the tall grass. "Okay, I want to know where you came from before Autumn and I found you. Before—" I tapped my watch and traced a broad arc through the air to indicate the past. "—you—" I pointed at her. "—came here," I finished, pointing at the abbey.

She glanced behind her as if expecting to see another person in the abbey. When she turned back she was frowning.

"That's really great, Leon," I muttered furiously. "Gave up your hands to *Endless Saga* and didn't bother to learn a stitch of Japanese. Bravo."

I closed my eyes and took a few calming breaths. I could almost hear my dad telling me that God wouldn't have put Shin in my path if it was impossible for me to help her.

"Before—you—came here," I attempted again, performing an even more exaggerated encore of my charades, "where did you come from?" I pointed all around myself and raised my palms in a questioning gesture.

Her frown became more calculating.

"Yes, good," I encouraged. "Where were you? Did you come from Cologne? That would be a heck of a walk but it might explain why you were outside for so long. Was it Cologne? Köln?" I repeated, using the city's German name.

She glanced around, looking uncertain once more.

Realistically I had no right to hope that she could respond to questions that required answers more complicated than Yes or No. And then only if I was lucky or particularly clever in the way I asked.

"I've got it," I said. "Shin."

"Ree-yong," she responded severely, apparently to show that we were on the same page.

"The person who hit you—" I made a fist and slowly pantomimed punching myself in the eye, then pointed at her. "Where was he?" I stared around theatrically, raising my palms. "Cologne? Tokyo? New York?"

Wonderful comprehension filled Shin's eyes. She raised her arm and pointed over my shoulder.

Cold excitement swept through me. "St. Goar?" I pointed the same direction she had and pantomimed another punch. "The person who hit you was in St. Goar?"

Her head bobbed again. Without taking her black eyes from mine she said, very clearly, "Seinto Go-wah."

3

My first thought was to rush right to the police to demand they track down and arrest the maniac who had hurt Shin so badly. Even if Shin did not know his identity, she would almost certainly be able to identify him in a criminal lineup, assuming they had criminal lineups in Germany.

The problem with that course of action, however, became apparent as I imagined striding into the St. Goar police station with Shin at my side. The nurses at the hospital might not have worried too much that Shin had no identification or papers but what would the police say? Would they want to keep her at the station until she could get new papers from the Japanese Embassy in Berlin?

Even worse, what if Shin had never had papers to begin with? She didn't seem to have gone to the authorities herself, after all. Would the German police put her in jail or simply deport her?

"We're going to Klaus and Greta's," I announced.

Shin, who had been watching me expectantly, raised her eyebrows.

"My host parents," I said, knowing and hating how useless my words were. I jerked my head toward town and held out my hand. "You ready to go?"

A pleasant little explosion took place in my stomach when Shin took my hand, as if a flock of sparrows were using my insides as a birdbath. But when I began to walk she pulled me back toward her. "*Chamkan manyo.*"

"What's up?" I said and immediately cleared my throat to cover the fact that my voice had cracked.

She brought my right hand up to her face and seemed to study it. After a moment she repeated the exercise with my left hand.

"Everything okay? I didn't wear my gloves last night. Maybe I should have."

Shin must have understood my nervous expression because she gave me an encouraging smile. "*Koktchong maseyo.*"

"Uh, yeah. Thanks. You ready to go then?"

Shin didn't hold my hand on the long walk to Klaus and Greta's but she seemed more at ease now that she knew I wasn't going to dump her at the abbey. On the outskirts of town she stopped me to point at a garden adorned with shiny colored balls on the ends of long sticks.

"*Ige mwoyeyo materia?*" she asked. This must have been funny because she giggled.

"My grandma has those in her vegetable garden," I explained, laughing also without knowing why. "They're supposed to scare birds away or something. I guess you probably don't see gardens in people's yards if you're from Tokyo or some other big city. I'm sure I'd be just as lost in a place like that as you are here."

We started walking again. "Grandma would love you. She goes to an acupuncturist twice a month for her lumbago. Dad might not be so cool," I mused. "Not that he's racist or anything but he gets all weird whenever he talks to the Indonesian family that goes to our church. Like they're from the moon or something."

Shin was nodding vaguely without really listening. I didn't mind. We crossed onto Oberstraße where Klaus and Greta lived, bringing the river into view. Shin watched a crammed river ferry swing ponderously around to dock at the St. Goar pier half a mile to the southeast, her mouth slightly open.

"Mom would get it," I resumed. "She's big into signs from God and things that are 'meant to be.' I bet she'd even recognize you the way I did. She watched me play Endless Saga sometimes when she was in her parents-should-be-hip-and-involved-in-their-kids'-entertainment phase. Here we are," I said, stopping at the little stairway leading up to Klaus and Greta's front yard.

Shin glanced unsurely at me but started up toward the house. Before she had reached the top step Greta emerged from the front door. I could tell right away something was wrong.

"*Der Klaus hat gerade angerufen,*" she said apologetically. "*Deine Freundin darf nicht hier bleiben.*"

I'd become so used to translating for Autumn that I did it automatically for Shin even though she couldn't understand English any better than German. "She says you can't stay here. *Warum denn?*" I asked Greta.

She explained that Klaus had informed Frau Werner about the situation with Shin—how Autumn and I had discovered her, bruised, semiconscious, and sheltering in the abbey—and that he and Greta were planning to house the girl until her identification could be sorted out. But Frau Werner had apparently forbidden Klaus from taking in a stray foreigner who had no papers and who had apparently been involved in a crime.

"Frau Werner works for a church!" I spluttered, so outraged I couldn't even think of how to say it in German. How many times had I heard my Dad preach on the chapter in Matthew that says we are called take the best care of the least of us?

Greta seemed to understand what I was thinking. She squeezed my arm gently. "*Tut mir Leid, mein Junge.*"

I expected Greta to go back inside now that she had delivered her terrible news but she continued to stand on the sidewalk outside her front door. After a moment I realized she must be blocking the door to make sure I wouldn't try to bring Shin into the house despite Frau Werner's decree.

Shin was watching Greta and me cautiously, aware that both of us were agitated but not sure why. I saw Greta's eyes flit over Shin's face. She made her familiar soft cluck of sympathy. However that sympathy apparently didn't extend to inviting Shin inside.

"*Danke,*" I told Greta numbly. I turned my back on her, recalling and now agreeing darkly with what Mrs. Miller had told our class about how German people can sometimes seem emotionally cold to Americans.

I touched Shin's shoulder to indicate that we were leaving. Greta, still clucking, shuffled back inside the house and latched the door.

Shin followed me back down the little stairway to the sidewalk before I stopped again. Where did I think I was going? I didn't know anyone else in St. Goar and to make matters worse Frau Werner's unwillingness to let Klaus and Greta host Shin even for a few days had confirmed my paranoia that the police might take Shin into custody if they learned about her.

"So it's Frau Werner we have to convince," I told Shin bracingly.

She was studying me with an almost Autumn-like shrewdness, as if she could tell I was barely holding myself together.

"Look, it makes sense that you're supposed to stay here," I insisted. "I wasn't able to get a service assignment because of my hands. Then you showed up and fixed my hands. You also obviously need help—you need someone to speak to the Germans for you, which I can do. See? It all fits."

But of course she didn't see. I might as well have been yelling *blah blah blah.*

"You're my service assignment," I said firmly. "Frau Werner will understand that."

"Leon!"

I spun around, startled. Autumn had just stepped into view around the corner where Oberstraße angled west toward downtown.

"What are you doing here already?" I snapped, wondering why her sudden appearance annoyed me.

She shrugged. "They showed us around the greenhouse and then let us come home early. We'll do a full day tomorrow. Elise said she was going to take another nap. I think she's trying to sleep away her homesickness. Hi," she added brightly to Shin, who smiled and offered a shallow bow by way of greeting.

And then it hit me: I didn't want to share Shin with anyone. Her safety was *my* concern, *my* service assignment. Autumn's voice rang through my mind: *You've got a real damsel in distress thing, don't you?* The fact that she seemed to be right didn't do anything to temper my annoyance.

Autumn came to a halt in front of us. Her smile faded. "What happened?"

"What makes you think—"

"Come on, Leon, you're an open book," Autumn said impatiently. "So?"

I glared at her but nothing could be gained by keeping her in the dark. First I recounted what Greta had told me about Frau Werner forbidding her and Klaus to host Shin, and finished by describing my plan to go to the church to see if I could change Frau Werner's mind.

"Won't work," Autumn said at once. "These Germans treat rules the way my dad used to treat the upholstery in his Mercedes. There's no way Frau Werner will bend on a rule this big."

"So what do you suggest?" I demanded. "Or are you only good at pointing out what won't work?"

Autumn stared at me levelly.

I took a deep breath. "I'm sorry. I'm just really worried."

"Apology accepted," Autumn said, her voice only slightly cooler than normal. "And I do understand. I know what she means to you."

You can't, I thought.

"Which is why," Autumn continued, "I'm going to buy her a hotel room here in town. She can stay there as long as she needs."

"What?"

"Well, you'll probably have to choose the best place and make the reservation or whatever, but I'll be the financial arm of our little partnership."

I blinked. "A hotel?"

"That hamster wheel in your brain is going to have to spin a little faster, Leon. We've both got the afternoon off, I've got a bank account full of money to burn, and Shin needs a place to stay. Now do you know of any hotels in St. Goar or should I get my guidebook?"

"Uh, there might be some near the town square," I said.

Autumn nodded briskly. "I'll get my book. You guys wait here."

She hopped up the stairs to Klaus and Greta's house and disappeared inside. Shin seemed to understand that we were going to wait for her because she sat down on the bottom step, watching the river.

I stood beside her, feeling utterly poleaxed. How could Autumn, who didn't speak more than ten words of German, seem more at ease in St. Goar than I was? Staring out at the many boats skating and buzzing across the surface of the river, some fighting the current and others gliding along with it, I suddenly found them an apt metaphor for both our lives. Except that Shin and I had fallen out of our boats and were completely at the river's mercy.

And who was tossing us a life preserver? Autumn Springer, the girl who most guys at school had simultaneously lusted after and dismissed as an amoral slut; the girl who my mother said only knew one way to relate to boys.

The door clicked behind us. I turned to see Autumn striding down the little sidewalk wearing a cloudy expression.

"What's wrong?"

"Nothing," she said. But before I could contradict her she exploded, "Did you know Greta speaks English?"

"I thought she might understand a little," I admitted. "Why? What'd she say?"

"She saw me counting money on my way out the door and asked if I was skipping work to go to the bar again. She hopes I'm not going to waste my opportunity to learn about work and family in Germany because many people, like the sweet girl outside—" She nodded at Shin. "—never get that chance."

"Greta said that?"

Autumn had already opened her guidebook to the pages relating to St. Goar. "So where do we want to look first? You said something about the town square, right? Did you mean the *Marktplatz?*"

"Hang on." I grabbed her arm. Distantly it occurred to me that I wouldn't have been able to do something as dexterous as grabbing anyone's arm twenty-four hours ago. "Did you tell her you have the afternoon off and you're helping Shin and me?"

She rolled her eyes. "Of course not, Leon. She didn't really think I was skipping work. She just wants me to know she has her eye on me. I've had enough lectures like that from teachers, boyfriends' moms, and my own father to recognize one when I hear it."

"That's ridiculous," I said, uncomfortably aware that, had I ever dated Autumn, my own mother would probably have given her a similar speech. "You're the one who's helping Shin because she and Frau Werner won't."

I leapt up the stairs and was preparing to charge into the house when Autumn spoke again. "Leon, don't." She didn't sound angry or resentful now. "There are some battles you can't fight for me, okay?"

"But—"

"And she's right. If I hadn't gone to that bar last night you wouldn't have all those stitches. Let's just find Shin a place to stay. Come on, sweetie," she added to Shin. They started walking toward downtown, Autumn's face mostly hidden behind the open guidebook.

Shin glanced back at me. "Ree-yong?"

I jumped down to the sidewalk. "Right behind you."

4

The temperature in the *Marktplatz* seemed to have risen twenty degrees since Shin and I had passed through this morning. The metal tables and chairs that had sprawled empty across the square earlier were now occupied with tourists attempting to keep cool with ice cream sundaes and glasses of foaming beer.

Despite the amount of people clogging the square, the three of us drew a great deal of attention. A group of college-age guys hollered something at Autumn in a language that might have been Russian, while most eyes followed Shin and myself. Mothers of young children in particular seemed unable to look away from our bandages. I couldn't decide whether they felt sorry for us—perhaps wondering where our own mothers were—or thought we had some weird skin disease we might pass to their kids.

"All right," Autumn said, digging her book out of her backpack as she walked. "The book says you can get a nice single room with breakfast at a place called Hotel Schwarzer Bär...the Difficult Bar Hotel?" she frowned, attempting to translate. "That can't be right."

"Black Bear," I corrected, pointing at a white five-story building with orange and magenta flowers growing from iron troughs below every window. A wooden sign swung quaintly over the front doors, painted with a lumbering black bear above the hotel's name. "Let's check it out."

But before we'd covered half the distance to the hotel we heard raised voices at one of the restaurants to our right.

"Look bro, I paid for this already!"

Autumn groaned. "Did that sound like Hat to you?"

I nodded, wondering if I was doomed to hear familiar voices shouting all summer. Autumn, Shin, and I veered right and waded between tables, excusing ourselves in three different languages to lunching tourists.

"*Es kostet weniger!*" a second and much deeper voice was saying to Hat.

"Look, I don't speak Spanish or whatever!" Hat said. "English or German, *por favor.*"

"He is speaking German," I said loudly.

Hat's head snapped around, his expression flickering between relief and irritation. He was holding the largest ice cream cone I had ever seen, which was melting in the sun, spattering the sidewalk with bright pink spots.

Beside him, looking even more annoyed, was a short man with a deeply tanned face and a thick black mustache. A tray of empty ice cream glasses balanced on one hand and a leather money belt around his waist suggested he was a waiter.

"*Entschuldigung,*" I said to the man. "*Er ist ein Bekannter von mir. Darf ich helfen?*"

The little man threw a disgusted glance up at Hat but began explaining what had happened in rapid, accented German. I guessed from the green, white, and red flags in the windows of the restaurant that he was Italian.

"He says you bought your ice cream at the window," I told

Hat, still listening carefully. "And then you sat down at one of their outdoor tables."

"Yeah, and I paid for it," Hat said hotly. "Is he saying—"

But Autumn shushed him while the Italian man continued speaking.

"It sounds," I said slowly, "like there are two different prices. One for the window and one for sitting down at the table. The window one must be a lot cheaper."

"That's the dumbest crap I've—" Hat began, but Autumn shushed him again. "You know what? To hell with this. I'm out."

He turned his back on all of us and stalked away, leaving a trail of fat pink drips on the cobblestone. Other patrons were openly staring between Hat and the glowering waiter. I apologized to the waiter, who still looked angry but seemed to regret how the situation had ended. He disappeared into the ice cream parlor.

Autumn sighed. "Should we go after him?"

"I think he'll be okay," I said. "He's probably had customers who didn't know the rules before."

"Not the waiter," Autumn giggled. "I meant Hat. He seemed pretty upset."

"Right!" I said uncertainly. "But I thought you didn't like—"

"If you want the measure of a person, you must look at how well they treat their inferiors, not their equals," she said with the mock gravitas of someone quoting an old lesson. "It's something like that anyway."

"Book of Matthew, right?" I asked, setting off with her in the direction Hat had gone. "I was just thinking about that earlier."

"No, *Harry Potter and the Goblet of Fire*." Autumn tapped the side of her nose. "Best book in the series."

We walked along in silence, winding between groups of tourists huddled around storefronts and postcard displays. Shin stayed closed behind us, displaying none of her previous enthusiasm for sightseeing.

"You were joking, right?" I asked Autumn. "About Hat being your inferior?"

"Yes, Leon," she said dryly. "I may act like a bitch sometimes but I can't fool myself into thinking I'm better than anyone else."

"You are," I said. Seeing her stiffen, I quickly added, "Not a b—b-word. I just mean you're better than you think you are. You offered to help Shin when no one else would."

She didn't seem to know what to say.

"Greta shouldn't have said that stuff to you."

Walking slightly behind her I saw her cheeks redden but I couldn't read her expression. A few moments later she pointed up the street.

"There he is. Jeez, did he eat that entire ice cream cone already? That thing was the size of my head."

Hat was in front of an athletic store, picking listlessly through an outdoor rack of soccer jerseys. He scowled as we approached.

"What are you guys doing here?" he growled.

"We wanted to make sure you're all right," I said.

Hat's scowl deepened. He batted a jersey aside and pretended to look at the next one.

"A few of us made plans to have supper at a pizza place Elise and I found this morning," Autumn told him coolly. "Leon thought you might want to go but if you're too awesome for us…"

She made to turn away. I frowned at her quizzically. This was the first I'd heard about the pizza restaurant. She gave her head a tiny shake.

"No! I mean, that's cool I guess," Hat said magnanimously. He was obviously attempting to recover his usual bravado. "What are you guys up to now? And who is that?" he added, finally seeming to notice Shin.

"Long story," Autumn said before I could explain. "We'll tell you tonight at supper. We're meeting at seven in the *Marktplatz*."

Without another word to him she headed back up the street

toward Hotel Schwarzer Bär. I waved goodbye to Hat and followed her, Shin on my heels. I wondered which of us understood less of what just happened.

The crowds had been building steadily all morning and now reached a terminal density. I was forced to turn sideways a few times between big groups of people just to keep up with Autumn. None of us even tried to speak until we reached the doorstep of the Hotel Schwarzer Bär.

Autumn dug under her shirt for her money belt and extracted five €100 notes. "Will that be enough for a few days?"

"I sure hope so," I said, goggling the money. It was more than I had brought for food and souvenirs for the whole summer.

Autumn pushed briskly into the hotel, and Shin and I followed. The lobby seemed especially dim after the glare of sunshine outside, with a low ceiling of some heavy, dark wood.

"*Guten Tag,*" Autumn said to the bearded man at the counter.

"English, yes?" the man replied. His eyes, practically invisible under great steel-colored flyaway eyebrows, flitted over Shin's and my bandaged faces. "You are wanting a room with *Dusche und WC?*"

"Excuse me?" Autumn said. "What do y—"

"It means a shower and toilet," I hissed in her ear.

"Oh," Autumn said, flustered.

"*Einzelzimmer mit WC und Dusche,*" I answered for her.

"*Siebzig Euro pro Nacht,*" the man said.

"*Also, eine Woche bitte. Ist das Frühstück im Preis inbegriffen?*"

"*Ja, ist inbegriffen,*" the man said.

Autumn was giving fitful little grunts of displeasure beside me.

"*Eine Woche,*" I confirmed.

The man pecked at a keyboard behind the desk with the same distrustful air as my grandfather checking his e-mail. After a few minutes a printer below the counter spat out a bill for €490.

"*Amerikaner?*" the man asked. I nodded. "*Warum können Sie so gut Deutsch?*"

Autumn snatched the paper out of his hand, scrawled her name across the bottom and handed over the five €100 notes. The man made change and passed it to her along with a key on a heavy wooden key ring. "*Bitte sehr.* The room is on the floor above. Breakfast begins at seven o'clock!" he called as she stalked away from the desk.

"*Vielen Dank,*" I said.

The man watched us leave, eyebrows continuing to twitch interestedly.

Autumn had already unlocked the room and was holding the door open for us when we reached the top of the narrow staircase. The room shared the same low, dark ceiling and cream colored walls as the hotel lobby. A cozy single bed rested against the wall below the room's only window, which offered an impressive view of Rheinfels Castle.

"Pretty swanky," I told Shin.

Taking my hand for balance, she crawled on her knees across the bed and stared delightedly out the window. "*Nomu choayo.*"

"Hey Autumn, I think she likes it," I laughed.

Autumn wasn't smiling. "Leon, did you ever think that maybe you're the one who thinks everyone is inferior to you?"

"What?"

"In the last few days you haven't let anyone do anything for themselves. As soon as anything remotely difficult happens you jump in with your perfect German to save the day. Like you're our Dad or something."

Something simultaneously hot and cold seemed to be washing over my scalp. She couldn't mean what she was saying. It was too unjust. I'd saved her life two nights ago.

"I'm just trying to help."

"That's what you say," Autumn agreed icily, "but it's not the whole truth. You get off on it. I can tell."

"Get off on it?"

"Why else would you refuse help from all those people yesterday when we were carrying her to the hospital? You've got this idea that God put her—" she pointed at Shin "—me, and Hat in your life so you can steer us away from danger like we're retarded puppies or something."

"That's not true."

"Oh, that's right," she jeered. "Hat and I are the puppies. Shin is, what, your perfect soul mate that all the sensitive Christian boys at New Canaan were hoping to meet so they could finally French kiss a girl without going to hell? Is that why you keep holding her hand?"

I dropped Shin's hand instinctively as if I'd been touching a stovetop burner. She stared between Autumn and me, castle view forgotten. Autumn's chest was heaving. Hectic pink patches had risen in her cheeks. Her eyes, however, were as clear and penetrating as ever.

Then something clicked into place and I suddenly thought I might understand our relationship even better than Autumn did. "I was being honest when I told you I would have helped anyone the way I helped you with that big German guy. It's not my fault your feelings got hurt when you realized it was true."

Autumn's perfect rosebud lips parted in outrage but she didn't seem to have an answer. Her silence was all the confirmation I needed.

"I'm going to go talk to Frau Werner like I should have done the moment I found out she wouldn't let Shin stay with the Holzes. I'll meet you here before we go to the pizza place if you still want me along." I turned to Shin. "I'll be back, okay?"

Neither she nor Autumn said anything as I left the room and latched the door behind me.

5

My feet carried me across town to the St. Goar Mennoniten-Kirche while my brain laboriously relived the scene with Autumn back in the hotel room. I felt sure I'd been right about the reason she had gotten so upset so quickly.

What had me shaking from head to toe with shame and anger as I walked was not Autumn's leering face as she accused me of treating her like a "retarded puppy," but her casual mockery of Shin's importance to me. I knew full well how pathetic it was that my only friends for most of high school had been characters in a video game. I'd admitted as much to Autumn.

But the fact that she knew what *Endless Saga* and Salvia meant to me should have made her realize Shin's presence in St. Goar simply couldn't be coincidental. To think otherwise would be what my dad called "scorn-again Christianity," the arrogant notion that human beings were so skilled at shaping our own existence that God didn't need to engage directly in our lives anymore.

Just pay attention, my dad had insisted in more sermons than

I could count, and God's gentle guidance would be both obvious and constant. Well, now I knew from experience that Dad had been right. Though in the case of Shin's appearance in St. Goar, God's influence seemed less like gentle guidance and more like shouting in my ear. Let Autumn sneer about soul mates and holding hands.

As I turned up the sidewalk to the St. Goar Mennoniten-Kirche a yellow Citroën hatchback about the size of a clown car in a circus act pulled up to the curb beside me. The engine shut off and the doors on either side swung open. Frau Werner rose from the driver's seat and a much smaller boy in a baseball cap exited the passenger side. He began struggling to yank a backpack as large as he was from the back seat. Frau Werner stepped around the car and freed the backpack with a single heave.

"Good morning, Leon," she said pleasantly, as if she had expected to find me waiting for her here. "Shall we go inside?"

The kid shouldered the enormous pack and trotted up the sidewalk toward the church at Frau Werner's side, the top of his cap bobbing along at her elbow.

"Leon, this is Bernard Schwarzentruber," declared Frau Werner, pronouncing the strong German name with obvious relish.

"Bernie," the kid piped up, arching an eyebrow imperiously at the woman towering over him.

"Leon Martin." I shook his small hand, taking pleasure in the simple fact that I could participate in this custom once more. "Are you also doing a summer program here?"

"Same as you. Culture of Service thing through Mennonite Central Committee. Volunteer here for three months and get college credit on the side, right?"

"Same as me," I agreed, trying to hide my surprise. I would have put Bernie's age around twelve at the oldest.

"Leon, I assume you are here to speak to me?" Frau Werner asked.

"That's right. If you have time."

"I must telephone Bernard's host family to pick him up. Then you and I can talk. But first let us all go into the church." She held the door open. "It is very warm to be standing outside, yes?"

I gestured for Bernie to go through the door ahead of me, which he did, eyes flicking from my hands to the bandages on my forehead as he passed. "Frau Werner said your hands were messed up. She didn't mention your face."

Frau Werner stiffened guiltily but I didn't mind that she'd told him. The others in the group had already heard about my arthritis directly from me. Anyway, it didn't seem like nearly as big a deal now that Shin had basically cured it. I flexed my fingers unconsciously. How could Autumn not see God's influence in bringing Shin and me together?

"Actually my hands are all right today," I told Bernie. "The bandages are from an accident the other night. I cut my forehead, had to get a few stitches."

"Huh," said Bernie.

Frau Werner led us to her office, outside of which two folding chairs had been placed to create a waiting area. Bernie plopped gratefully into one of them, letting his huge backpack thump to the floor beside him. I took the other chair.

"I will be back in a moment, boys," Frau Werner assured us. She disappeared into her office.

Bernie immediately leaned over and rummaged in one of the side pockets of his backpack, withdrawing a sleek black bundle. He pressed a button on its side and a flat screen flickered to life in the middle of it. I thought it was a cell phone until I saw the familiar arrangement of buttons on its shiny face.

"Is that for games?"

Something in my voice must have given me away because Bernie arched his eyebrow again. "You a gamer?"

"Used to be."

He shrugged. "I've got all the consoles at home but Mom said

I could only bring one handheld to Germany with me. Gamicon Lite's got the best games."

The little screen had a surprisingly sharp picture. I watched him navigate the menu with mild interest that ramped up into seizure inducing shock when the words *Endless Saga* appeared next to an icon in the menu. "What—" I croaked, and cleared my throat before trying again. "What games do you have on there?"

"Mostly old-school stuff. I downloaded a bunch of role-playing games that should last me all summer. *Plume Knight, Aeon Quest, Endless Saga*—you know the drill. I got through like six hours of *Plume Knight* on the plane ride over here because the in-flight movies sucked."

"C-Could I see?"

"Course," he said, passing over the little black device carelessly.

Scarcely able to believe I wasn't dreaming, I laid my thumbs on either side of the gamepad, navigating the buttons easily despite trembling fingers. A tiny video icon next to the *Endless Saga* listing was playing the opening cinematic. I clicked the icon and the screen flashed momentarily while the game loaded. My heart was pounding in my throat.

Get a grip. It's just a game.

But I couldn't get a grip. Not emotionally, at least—my hands were certainly gripping the Gamicon Lite just fine. When Bernie reached over I had a mad urge to jerk it away from him. But he only pressed a button to turn up the sound.

"The speakers are sort of terrible. I have headphones if you want."

I shook my head, still staring at the screen. Letters grew like vines across the screen, spelling *Endless Saga*. Wrapped within the English title was the original Japanese text:

エンドレスサガ

Although I had seen this text hundreds of times without really paying attention, this time it seemed much more significant. I groped in my pocket for the little piece of paper on which Shin had written her name in three different alphabets. I understood now why the last one had looked familiar to me.

シンウンミュン

Autumn may have doubted whether Shin was actually Japanese but here was undeniable proof, written in the same letters as the title of my favorite game. Both names even seemed to share a symbol, the one that looked like a winking eye over a checkmark. I folded the paper and slid it carefully back into my pocket.

The game seemed to have grown tired of waiting for me to press Start. It began to cycle through a list of credits interspersed with images of each character that I drank in like photos of friends who had moved away. My heart, already jackhammering away, seemed to trip over itself when Salvia's picture appeared on the little screen, smiling shyly up at me between shining curtains of raven-black hair.

At last I pressed the start button and heard the familiar *ting* sound that meant the game was starting up. The tinny speakers Bernie had complained about erupted with Latin voices singing the game's main choral theme.

And then Salvia appeared on the screen once more, in motion this time, running across a mountain field full of yellow and pink flowers under a vast cloud strewn sky. The field in the game was the twin of the one on the outskirts of St. Goar—wild grass and flowers with hills and trees in the distance.

Frau Werner's door opened, wrenching me from the beautiful world locked behind that tiny screen.

"Bernard, your host parents will pick you up outside in a few minutes."

"Cool." He stood and heaved his pack onto his shoulder. To me he added, "You want to borrow that? I should probably be social my first day with the host family, right?"

"I shouldn't—"

"Well *I* shouldn't either. Go on, take it and remove temptation from my sight," he said, laying a skinny forearm dramatically across his eyes.

I decided Bernie was weird. But I also liked him. "Just for the afternoon. I can give it back to you tonight. The rest of the group is meeting in the *Marktplatz* at seven to go out for pizza. You're welcome to join us."

"Cool," he repeated. "Oh, before I forget..." He reached around and dug once more in the side pocket of his backpack. "The battery's almost dead. You'll need the power cord if you want to play more than an hour."

"I won't—"

"You might," he grinned, shoving the cord into my hands. "That's a European adapter so you can plug it right into the wall." He turned and shuffled down the hall toward the front door.

"Leon, I believe you have something to discuss?" asked Frau Werner.

With an effort I switched off the game. The Latin choir, still roaring out its chorus, cut off mid-phrase. And in that snap of silence I realized that Bernie and his video games weren't any more coincidence than Shin was. They were meant to remind me that while games had been the most important thing in my life for years they had also ruined me. Betrayed me.

I slid the Gamicon Lite into the big side-pocket of my cargo shorts. Real people mattered. Shin mattered. Just as surely as she had been brought to St. Goar to help me with my arthritis, I had been brought here to help solve her problem, whatever it might be. She was my service assignment.

"Yes," I told Frau Werner, "we have something to discuss."

6

Frau Werner led me into the controlled pandemonium of her office and directed me to sit. "You will take an early Kaffeezeit with me, yes?" she said.

"Thank you," I said, uncertain whether I'd just been given an invitation or an order.

She filled an electric teapot with a jug of water from a small refrigerator behind her desk and switched it on. A French press already full of dry coffee grounds stood on the shelf beside the teapot. Next she drew two large wedges of cheesecake from the refrigerator—leftovers from yesterday's failed party—and set them on the desk between us, complete with knife, fork, and folded cloth napkin, before taking her own seat. "The water will heat quickly. The coffee will be ready to drink in a few minutes."

"Thank you," I said again. I briefly considered switching languages; Frau Werner had seemed much more helpful and kind while we spoke German in yesterday's meeting. But no matter how she praised my German it didn't hold a candle to her English and I didn't want there to be any misunderstandings. "I think you know why I'm here."

She peered down at me. Even when seated she remained several inches taller. "You are not wearing your gloves today. Is our climate near the river beneficial to your arthritis?"

"No," I said, caught off guard. "The first night here my hands hurt worse than usual."

"So you believe it was the girl who eased your pain. Her name is Shin, yes? One moment..."

The electric teapot had already begun to hum loudly as if a clan of angry wasps lived inside it. She poured the boiling water into the French press.

"Autumn described to me this morning the way you discovered the injured Japanese girl. She also asked whether the girl could live with the Holzes."

"She did?" I asked, nonplussed. "Why would she do that?"

Frau Werner's eyebrows rose. "She seemed to think it was your wish. I considered the matter very carefully. However, it is impossible, as I told Herr Holz when he stopped by."

"But why is it impossible?" I demanded. "If the church won't help her, who will?"

She sat up even straighter, her expression suddenly hard. "Did I say the church would not help the girl? Naturally we will help her. However, the laws governing the housing of exchange students such as yourself do not cover undocumented foreigners. The likelihood that she is involved in sex trafficking makes her case even more complicated."

I was on my feet without realizing I had stood, my chair overturned on the floor. Frau Werner half rose from her own seat. She looked as startled as I felt.

"You must understand, Leon, Germany has one of the largest sexual tourism industries in all of Europe. Many young boys and girls are kidnapped all over the world and brought to Germany for that purpose. Or if they are not kidnapped they are lured here with a promise of money or schooling, only to discover that neither exists. And while they do make a great deal of money they are never permitted to keep enough of it to return home. In other words, they become indentured servants. Slaves."

I felt dizzy, sick. Shin a prostitute? Not brought here by God but by some kind of international sex ring?

"That's impossible," I heard myself say.

"In my position as director of the Culture of Service training program I have worked closely with law enforcement offices in Nordrhein-Westfalen, Hessen, Rheinland-Pfalz, and Saarland. I am sorry to say I have seen such things happen in every state," Frau Werner said tiredly. She reached out and pushed down the plunger on the French press. A golden froth rose to the surface of the coffee inside. "So you see, the circumstances I described are quite possible. An ugly truth is still the truth."

But already my stunned mind was calling up yesterday's conversation between Nurse Gabi and Autumn. I seized upon the memory like a gasping swimmer on a hunk of driftwood in a turbulent river.

"The nurse! The nurse at the hospital—her name was Gabi—she told us Shin hadn't been…"

I couldn't bring myself to say the word "rape."

"…forced. You know, sexually."

Frau Werner had filled one mug and was pouring the second, but at this she paused. "Perhaps there is some good news after all. But you must see how the situation is more complicated than whether or not I wish to house the girl with one of my families. If she has been kidnapped or brought to Germany with false promises of wealth or opportunity, then the most important thing is for her to return to her family and her country."

I slowly turned my chair upright and sat down. "I'm sorry I overreacted."

"You are young," said Frau Werner tersely, topping off the second mug. "And the young are passionate. Please," she added, indicating the cheesecake and coffee on my side of the desk.

I took a bite of cake, mostly to be polite. I'm sure it would have tasted very good if my stomach had been in any mood to accept food. Frau Werner ate her cake as well, dividing it into neat, bite-size squares with a knife and fork. Neither of us spoke while we ate. When she had finished the last square of cake and swallowed the last dregs of coffee from her mug she dabbed at the corners of her mouth with her napkin.

"I am also grateful that Autumn was so careful about upholding German laws," she said, as if our conversation had not stopped for several minutes. "She has made the matter of sheltering this girl much simpler than I could have hoped."

"Sorry?" I said, setting my own empty mug into its saucer.

She stifled a quiet belch in her napkin. "*Begnadigen Sie mein Deutsches,*" she said with a very un-Frau-Werner-ish chuckle. The cake seemed to have greatly improved her spirits. "I was simply expressing my gratitude that Autumn made certain she would not break any German laws by purchasing a hotel room for the girl."

"How did she do that, exactly?"

"When I explained that none of my families could host the girl, Autumn offered to find the girl lodging with her own money. She also wanted to be sure that staying in a hotel without a passport would not get the girl into any trouble. I assured her it would not. I offered to help but she said she would do it on her own. She is a proud girl, I think."

"She is." I was thinking again of our argument. Was Autumn right? Did I "get off" on helping people? If so, I wasn't very good at it. Sure, I had taken the blow meant for Autumn in the bar, and I'd stopped the waiter at the ice cream shop from yelling at Hat any more than he already had. Then, at the hotel, Autumn had clearly struggled to understand the manager but had I really needed to intervene on her behalf? Of course I hadn't.

As for Shin, she'd helped me immeasurably with my arthritis but what had I actually done for her? I couldn't have carried her to the hospital without Autumn's help. My "perfect" German hadn't been up to more than a couple questions from the hospital staff—their English, like Frau Werner's, had been head and shoulders above my German. And I certainly couldn't have paid for the room at Hotel Schwarzer Bär with the meager bit of money I'd saved up for the summer.

All of a sudden I felt helpless. Pointless.

Frau Werner was saying something.

"What?" I asked bleakly.

"Was Autumn able to find a hotel or does she require help?"

"She bought Shin a room at the Hotel Schwarzer Bär."

"An excellent choice," Frau Werner said, pleased. "The girl will be comfortable while we sort out her identity. That is as much as we could have asked for."

I stood. "Thank you for the coffee and cake."

Frau Werner frowned. "You are welcome. I will contact you as soon as I find a service assignment. You may still visit anytime."

I nodded dimly. More than anything I wanted to be out of this office, away from people. To escape. As I plodded out of the office and down the church's dark hallway, Bernie's Gamicon Lite banged softly against my thigh from inside my pocket as if trying to remind me there was a familiar, welcoming place to which I could escape with the push of a button.

7

Klaus and Greta's house was silent and empty when I returned and I couldn't have been happier about it. The last thing I wanted to deal with was Greta's tense questioning about what we had done with Shin, or her dour editorials about Autumn's attitude.

I vaulted up the narrow staircase to my room and flopped onto the hard futon. The travel alarm on the nightstand read 3:20. I still had over three hours before I had to face Autumn again. And face her I would. That wasn't even a question because Autumn would be with Shin. More than that, she had a right to be with Shin. Perhaps more of a right than I had.

The self-disgust that had threatened to overwhelm me in Frau Werner's office rose like hot bile in my chest. I stuffed a hand into the cargo pocket of my shorts and pulled out the Gamicon Lite. Was this really a road I wanted to go down again? Hadn't video games—this very video game—brought upon me a lifetime of pain and disability?

The Gamicon Lite flashed like a black mirror in the afternoon light glaring through the open skylight above the bed. I saw my own face reflected in the screen, pale, brooding, and miserable. And beneath those emotions a foundation of raging self-pity. I saw it as clearly as I saw the white bandages taped to my forehead.

"Screw it," I told my reflection and jabbed the power button. Although I'd never played a game on a portable device like this it felt intoxicatingly familiar in my hands. I plugged in Bernie's power cord, selected *Endless Saga* from the list of games, and instantly became lost in the Latin choral music, in the beautiful girl in the flower-strewn field.

The room around me melted away. I ceased being Leon Martin and became Typhoon Darkwater, student of the Bedlam Forest Mercenary Academy. I made my way across through forests of Bedlam and across a wide sea to a town under siege, taking care to train Typhoon and the others in my battle party up to Level 25 before reaching the first enemy boss atop a massive radio tower.

I saved my game after the battle, remembering that I could gain triple experience points in the upcoming scene if I played correctly and would retry if I failed. I rolled my head on my shoulders, grimacing at the pops and cracks coming from my neck, while the save-bar filled on the screen. A hot, gritty ache had returned to my knuckles. The bones of my forearms seemed laced with tiny threads of molten glass that promised to grow into thick ropes by nightfall...

And speaking of nightfall, the view outside my skylight was now tinged with the faint pink of twilight.

Appalled, I glanced at the clock, which read 8:10. I'd been playing for almost five hours straight. Klaus and Greta's voices drifted up the staircase from the kitchen, punctuated with clinking of silverware on dishes. Had I remembered to tell them we would eat supper elsewhere? Would Autumn and the other still be at the restaurant?

I switched off the Gamicon Lite, rolled up the cord, jammed

both into my pocket, and slid stiffly off the bed. After a quick detour to the restroom I dashed downstairs into the kitchen, startling Klaus and Greta.

"*Nur mit der Ruhe,*" Greta admonished.

"The Autumn telephoned to say you are eating the pizza tonight with your group, yes?" Klaus boomed brightly.

"Yes," I panted. "Did she tell you where the restaurant is?"

With one of her disapproving clucks, Greta gave me directions to the pizza place in rather pointed German. It sounded like it wasn't far from the *Marktplatz.* I wished them both a good night and left the kitchen at a run, with Greta's reproving shouts following me out the front door.

I continued running all the way to the *Marktplatz.* By the time I got there the stitches in my forehead stung with sweat and a hot ache had risen in my side to rival the throbbing fire in my hands and wrists. I deserved all of it and more. What had I been thinking, reopening myself to *Endless Saga?* Now I understood why alcoholics who had quit drinking were called "recovering" rather than "cured." Once an addict, always an addict.

I located the street on which Greta had said I would find the restaurant and I jogged another block before I saw it. Like the ice cream parlor in the *Marktplatz,* much of the seating was outside. A low iron fence divided the patio from the public sidewalk, studded every few feet with antique lamps that cast yellow globes of light in the humid night air.

Autumn, Hat, Shin, Elise, and Bernie were seated at a round wrought iron table. Pizza crusts and greasy napkins lay scattered across the table like the remains of a hyenas' feeding frenzy, along with several beer mugs and wine glasses.

Shin spotted me and called, "Ree-yong!" She was still wearing the new pink t-shirt that said *Kein Problem!* and the tan capri pants Nurse Gabi had given her at the hospital. She also now wore a floppy sunhat that Autumn must have bought for her this afternoon while I played video games. Another wave of hot guilt washed over me.

Bernie and Elise, who were facing the other direction, turned in their seats and waved. Bernie wore a knowing smile that I tried to ignore.

"'Ree-yong'?" Hat repeated loudly. Now that I was closer to the table, I realized at least three of the beer mugs were in front of him. "That's awesome."

Autumn held a glass of red wine in one hand but seemed far more in control of herself. She spared Hat a single disdainful glance that suggested she regretted inviting him. "I didn't think you'd come," she told me.

"I was…I fell asleep. I'm really sorry." I hoped she would understand that I wasn't just apologizing for being late. "You all met Bernie, I see."

"Yup." Bernie was definitely grinning now. "Good nap?" he asked with a ludicrous wink.

I chose to ignore this also. I tried to pick up a chair from another table, but it was made of heavy iron like the table and my hands lacked the strength to lift it.

Elise got up and dragged the chair over to the table. "Here you go."

My cheeks burned. "Thanks."

Shin was staring at my hands with a troubled expression. She obviously thought her acupuncture treatment should have lasted longer.

"You missed quite a show," Hat announced, cocking his thumb and forefinger at me like a pistol. "Autumn reserved this table and ordered us pizza in perfect German. *Deutsch-o perfecto.*" He slung his arm roughly around her shoulders.

Autumn lifted his arm off of her, firmly setting it back against his side. "Unfortunately," she said resignedly, "our friend Ronald knows the German word for beer."

Hat leaned forward and whispered, "It's pronounced *beeeeeer.*"

Bernie was still smirking, though now at Hat instead of me. Elise kept glancing at the restaurant's front door as if nervous the wait staff might throw us out for being unruly.

Shin on the other hand watched Hat with plain disgust. Her expression reminded me of my Aunt Carrie's tabby, Roxanne, which, whenever my dad tried to pet it, laid its ears flat and gave a single low growl before taking a swing at him.

"What happened to your hands, Leon?" Autumn asked. Her calm voice betrayed none of the effort she must have been expending to fend off Hat. He still held his fingers out like guns and was using them to poke her arms and side.

"I did something I shouldn't have," I said, reaching into my pocket for Bernie's Gamicon Lite.

"So that's why you were late," Hat said gleefully. "We all do it, Leonardo. Sometimes you just gotta polish the old stripper pole—hey!"

Autumn had reached over and pulled his beer out of reach. "I'd hoped you'd be a maudlin drunk," she said tiredly.

"Autumn knows what I'm talking about," Hat went on, once more tossing his arm carelessly around her neck. "It's like when I bought those pictures of her off the internet."

She stood, spinning gracefully out of his grasp. "I'll cover the tab tonight since I invited you all here."

Bernie's smirk faded. "I've got money."

"I do too," said Elise.

She was watching Hat with something like disgust now too, but it was nothing to match Shin's. I could almost hear her growling like my aunt's cat.

"Hey, come on, guys, I thought we were having fun," Hat said.

"One of us is," Autumn corrected him sweetly. To the others she said, "Pizza's on me tonight, end of story. Consider it my way of saying I'm pleased to meet you."

But as she turned to go inside Hat propelled himself to his

feet. I don't know if what he did next was on purpose or not, but he lurched toward her unsteadily, arms raised in front of him like Frankenstein's monster in an old horror movie, and grabbed her breasts from behind. She stumbled backward and both of them lost their balanced, toppling backward into his seat. Autumn thudded onto his lap with a high, surprised "*Oof!*"

We all jumped up but Shin reached Autumn's side first. Her hands flashed oddly in the soft glow of the streetlamps. A moment later the whole street echoed with a high, ear-splitting shriek. Diners and waiters began pouring out of the restaurant to see what had happened. My eyes danced from Autumn to Shin to Elise to determine which of them was making that awful scream. It was a frantic, desperate sound that surely must mean one of them had been mortally wounded.

But none of them seemed hurt. They were all staring at Hat. Autumn and Elise with horror and Shin with…satisfaction?

Suddenly I realized what those flashes in Shin's hands must have been. I looked down at Hat, dread gnawing a big empty hole in my abdomen, and saw what he was screaming about. His left arm dangled pointlessly at his side like a dead eel. A cluster of ornate needles jutted from the elbow.

He attempted to stand, using his right arm to push himself upright. But he overbalanced and fell against the side of his iron chair, spilling it and himself onto the sidewalk with a crash. The side of his head bounced off the cobblestones with an unpleasant, gritty thud. His left arm lay pinned under his body, limp and lifeless.

One of the waiters broke through the crowd and helped Autumn disentangle Hat from his chair. In the soft light of the antique lamps, Hat's face had turned a waxy yellow. One cheek still pressed against the sidewalk, eyes rolling madly in their sockets, he grabbed a fistful of the waiter's shirt. "She killed me, bro. If you find my arm, send it to my mother. She'll want something to bury."

And then he fainted.

DISC 3

1

A brief, confused silence followed Hat's loss of consciousness. Within seconds, however, the crowd of Germans who had poured out of the restaurant began muttering to one another. A few raised cell phones to their ears, probably calling the police. This didn't concern me nearly as much as the people who lifted their cell phones to take pictures. I wondered again whether there were criminal lineups in Germany. Well, nobody would need a lineup if even a handful of witnesses had clear photographs of Shin.

Autumn was still kneeling beside Hat, and after a moment I realized she was trying to shield Hat's body from view of the onlookers. She pulled the cluster of needles from Hat's arm with a single unceremonious yank. His whole body twitched. His eyes continued to roll back and forth under his eyelids as if he was having an intense dream.

"Get her out of here, Leon," Autumn hissed, surreptitiously holding the needles out to me. Their tips looked slick and black in the dim lighting.

I accepted them and carefully wiped them on the side of my shorts. None of the Germans seemed to have seen Shin's attack or the needles, including the waiter who had helped Autumn extricate Hat from his overturned chair. He was now facing the little knot of restaurant patrons with his arms out, looking for all the world like a TV cop performing crowd control. *Go on home, folks. Nothing to see here.*

A few superior chuckles drifted from the crowd but they were apparently content to obey the waiter and go back inside. The few who had taken pictures were now holding up their phones to their friends and grinning, amused at the images they had captured.

I didn't dare hand the needles back to Shin before we had left the restaurant patio lest some curious onlooker notice and snap another picture. If Hat needed to go to the hospital—had the St. Goar hospital ever dealt with so many foreigners in such a short time?—I didn't want the nurses to have any evidence to help them figure out what had made the patch of angry red punctures in his elbow.

"What did she do to him?" a small voice asked behind me. I turned to see Elise staring down at Hat, her wide, dark eyes taking up more of her face than ever.

"Badass," Bernie said approvingly.

"Leon!" Autumn said urgently. "Go, dammit. I'll take care of this and meet you back at the hotel."

I took Shin's hand and squeezed it to let her know we should get a move on. She fell into step at my elbow silently, docilely. I offered quiet goodbyes to Elise and Bernie—the latter had already sat back down and was unconcernedly slurping Fanta through a straw. As Shin and I reached the end of the iron fence around the restaurant's patio I heard him ask Elise, "You think Leon's pal also pulled that needle-jitsu on the punk who beat her up? Man, I wonder if that guy survived."

He was obviously joking but the blood turned to ice in my veins. I'd assumed Shin had been living in the abbey ruins to hide from the monster who had hit her. What if I'd gotten that part wrong? What if she'd killed the monster already and was actually hiding from the police?

A raucous shout echoed across the square ahead of us, accompanied by the clap of running footsteps. I tensed, imagining a brigade of police officers tramping toward us to arrest Shin. Before we could do more than duck into the arched doorway of a closed bakery, a group of young men—definitely not police officers—staggered into view around the corner, evidently playing a rather drunken game of tag. Shin and I remained huddled in the doorway while they passed, which they did at great volume and speed.

"So much for a quiet night in St. Goar, right?" I said, attempting to match Bernie's unconcerned, ain't-we-havin-a-ball attitude from earlier.

Shin gave one of her head bobs. And then her whole face seemed to crumple in on itself. Her lips pressed together so hard they turned white. Fat tears rolled down her cheeks in shining tracks.

"*Chib eh ka go shippo,*" she moaned, mashing her palms against her eyes as if trying to push the tears back inside her head.

The acupuncture needles tinkled softly to the ground as I grasped her wrists and pulled them back down to her sides. "Whoa, careful! That bruise is just starting to heal. You don't want to…you know…hurt it more."

She was staring up at me with such naked desperation that right then I would have done anything in the world to keep her from ever feeling hurt or unhappy again. Our bodies were very close inside the doorway, our faces inches apart. The small bumps of her breasts pressed against my chest, soft and firm and surprisingly warm through the thin fabric our t-shirts. I could feel her heart racing mere inches away from my own.

Something cataclysmic and wonderful was happening deep inside me. My face moved toward hers as if pushed by some outside force. Our lips brushed. Shin's whole body stiffened. Her arms twitched.

I opened my eyes—had I closed them?—and when I saw the look on Shin's face, my stomach took another of those deep swoops, though the sensation was anything but wonderful this time. Her expression was still wide open and desperate, but now tainted with shock.

Suddenly I saw myself through Shin's eyes: a gangly and awkward stranger who, yes, had shown her some level of kindness but now thought it "entitled him to a grope" as Autumn had so succinctly put it the other day.

I let go of her at once and knelt, hot-faced, to scrabble on the ground for the needles I'd dropped. I couldn't bear to look at her, to see that terrible shock again.

I am not like Hat.

I collected all of the needles and stood without looking up from the ground. "I'll take you back to the hotel."

Neither of us said anything on the short walk to the Schwarzer Bär. The chatter drifting around the tables in the *Marktplatz* seemed impossibly pleasant and carefree, the way birdsong must sound through the bars of a prison window.

"Here we are," I said, tugging open the heavy door of the hotel. I still couldn't make myself look at Shin.

I felt her small, searching fingers in my hand. Hope and excitement flitted through my stomach before I realized she was just retrieving her needles.

"*Ko mab sum ni da.*"

I thought I had heard this expression before, but I couldn't remember the context. Was it goodbye?

"Yeah," I mumbled. "I'm sorry I…"

But that was as far as I got. There was no way to finish the apology without making myself feel even worse about what I'd done. Not that I *should* feel any better about it. What had I been thinking?

Her fingers now drifted to either side of my face, drawing it up toward hers. I tried to turn away but she said sternly, "Ree-yong."

"I'm sorry," I repeated, forcing myself to meet her large, dark eyes.

"*Arigato gozaimashita,*" she said slowly and carefully. The Japanese term for "thank you." She even smiled a little when she said it.

She continued to hold my face and for an instant—I hated myself for wishing it—I thought she might kiss me. But the moment passed. She let her hands fall to her sides, turned, and disappeared into the hotel.

2

The first rays of daylight crawling across my futon from the skylight, accompanied by the clanking of pans down in the kitchen as Greta made breakfast, came as a relief. I had spent most of the night in a haze of haunted half-wakefulness and partially recalled nightmares. One in particular involved being chased down a dark alleyway by a slender, cadaverous creature with booming footsteps and shiny silver needles for teeth. Sleep had not returned after that.

On a positive note, I had at least remembered to put on my Thermoskin gloves before crawling into bed. My hands felt better than they had any right to feel after yesterday's *Endless Saga* marathon. A testament to Shin's acupuncture treatment more than the gloves, no doubt.

But that only brought my mind back to Shin. Had I really kissed her in that doorway last night? My first kiss…and a horrifying mistake. I would never forget her terrible, shocked expression the moment I had drawn away from her. Not that I had any right to forget.

"Idiot," I muttered, rubbing my palms against my eyes. The gloves' coarse stitching raked my eyelids. "Idiot."

Someone wrapped softly on my door. "Leon?"

I froze. Autumn might not be the last person I wanted to see this morning but she was a close second. She would want to talk about what had happened at the restaurant, which would lead to questions about whether Shin had been okay when I'd taken her back to the hotel. And I knew I wouldn't be able to hide the fact that something else bad had happened. Not from Autumn.

I lay completely still and tried to slow down my breathing. I even threw in a light snore for good measure.

She called dryly through the door, "I heard you talking to yourself a second ago."

I sighed. "Hang on, I need to put on some clothes."

The knob turned and Autumn strode in with her hands over her eyes. Although if anyone should have hidden their eyes, it was me. She was wearing the outfit she must have slept in, except the term "outfit" was rather generous. The shirt was another of her apparently endless supply of halter tops, but much older than the others, faded pink and thinner than Shin's hospital gown had been. Her shorts were shiny satin things that didn't quite cover her underpants.

Eyes still covered, she felt around the floor with the tips of her bare toes until she found the corner of my futon and sat down on it. "You decent yet?"

Was *I* decent?

"N-not yet," I said, snatching my cargo shorts off the floor and stuffing my legs into them under the covers. Autumn had already seen me without a shirt on the other day, but for some reason her current outfit made me feel more exposed. I slid out of bed and dug a fresh t-shirt out of my backpack. "Okay."

Autumn lowered her hands. "So last night was a disaster."

I froze. Could she already know? "What makes you say that?"

"Your girlfriend totally flipped out," she said as if it should have been obvious. "Did you figure out what set her off?"

"Oh!" I said. "Right, well I don't think she liked Hat touching your...you. And you obviously didn't like it very much either," I added, reddening as Shin's unhappy expression rose yet again in my memory.

Autumn noticed me blushing but for once she seemed to misunderstand. She folded her arms across her chest. "He was drunk. I don't think he would have been so bold sober."

"How does being drunk make it any better?" I demanded, positively wallowing in shame now. I *had* been sober.

"It doesn't," she said, surprised. "I'm just making an observation."

"And anyway, you just about took that one guy's head off in the bar the other night for doing the same thing."

"Hang on, that was not the same thing. Hat's like a little boy who's just discovered his pee-pee. The guy in the bar was scary. Like, kidnap and torture women in his basement because he hated his mother scary. There's a difference between a person who's annoying or disrespectful and a one who's dangerous. After last night I'm starting to wonder if maybe Shin can't tell that difference."

"I don't follow you."

"Look, I got hundreds of e-mails from guys who bought my pictures. Most of them were like Hat—repressed, immature, and sexually self-delusional. But not threatening. You wouldn't believe how many men seem to think they must be irresistible lovers simply by virtue of having sexual organs."

"Huh," I said uncomfortably. Did trying to kiss someone without permission put me into that last category? I pushed the question away.

"Anyway," Autumn went on, "there were only three types of men who ever actually scared me." She ticked them off on her fingers. "Religious nutcases who demonized all sexuality, men who hated themselves because they couldn't admit or didn't know they were gay, and men who were unknowingly drawn to pornography because they had been sexually abused. There's plenty of crossover between all three types, of course. The point is, they all scared me for the same reason: they hate women."

"So Shin thinks that Hat is the kind of guy who hates women? That's why she attacked him?"

"Not necessarily. I'm actually wondering if Shin lost control with Hat because she was abused herself, and because of that she hates all men. We know something bad happened to her recently. Those bruises on her face weren't from slipping on a loose stone in the abbey."

If that were the case, I thought, she would have attacked me too. Instead she had thanked me. But for what?

To Autumn I said, "She doesn't seem to hate me."

"Yeah, well, you're not like other guys."

"What's that supposed to mean?"

"Don't be so touchy," Autumn said lightly. "I only mean you're about safest guy I've ever been around. That's a good thing."

And a moment ago I'd thought I couldn't feel any worse about myself. "You ready for breakfast?" I asked tiredly.

"Do I look ready?" She snorted. "I had to come talk to you because I couldn't stop thinking about last night. I do feel better now."

She stood and stretched her arms luxuriantly over her head, yawning and bouncing on her toes. I tried to look away and found I couldn't.

At last she turned and padded out of my room. "Thanks for the chat."

"Sure," I said. My voice cracked and I coughed into my glove to cover it up.

"Tell Klaus and Greta I'll be down in a few minutes?" she called over her shoulder.

"Sure," I repeated.

I stared at the empty doorway for several moments. Not for the first time since arriving in Germany I wondered what exactly was happening to me. I had noticed pretty girls in school but I had never asked one out or, God help me, tried to kiss one. From somewhere deep in my mind I heard my dad's voice sternly insisting that looking at or thinking about a woman's body without her permission was equal to taking advantage of her physically.

He had not delivered this message from the pulpit, but directly to me when I was 14, getting ready to go to a pool party that the Bontrager family held every August for the church youth group. Convinced that I'd be unable to keep from looking at my female classmates in their bikinis if I went outside, I'd spent the entire afternoon in the kitchen helping Mrs. Bontrager prepare snacks. Admittedly, this hadn't really rectified the situation as Mrs. Bontrager had been wearing a bathing suit herself. Standing beside her at the kitchen counter I could have counted the freckles on her cleavage if I'd wanted to.

Then again, if Dad hadn't suggested I would be tempted to stare at the girls' bodies, would it have been an issue? The other boys in my class had mostly ignored the girls, instead spending the afternoon whapping each other with those foam floatation noodles and seeing who could make the biggest splash off the diving board.

Regardless, I had controlled myself that day. And if I'd been able do it then, while in the early throes of puberty, why couldn't I now?

But that was cowardly and idiotic. Dad had also taught me that self-control would come to anyone who tried hard enough.

My eyes fell on Bernie's Gamicon Lite, which I'd placed back on the nightstand last night when I'd realized that I had forgotten to return it. I considered slipping it into my pocket even though it was unlikely I would see Bernie today.

In the end I left the Gamicon Lite where it was. Self-control.

3

Klaus's round face was hidden behind a newspaper when I entered the kitchen. "*Guten Morgen, mein Sohn!*" he roared happily without lowering the paper.

I took this as a good sign. I had been half-worried that the incident at the pizza restaurant might show up in today's news. The *New Canaan Gazette* back home would have covered such an event with at least one news article and most likely a crotchety phone-in editorial about the decline of America's youth.

Greta greeted me rather more stiffly than she had done the previous mornings, whether because of our argument yesterday morning or the rambunctious manner in which I'd left the house last night I couldn't tell. Still, the breakfast of hard rolls and meats, cheeses, and jams was just as grand as usual.

When she poured Klaus's morning mug of *Kräutertee* he folded his paper and placed it in his lap like a large napkin. "So, you have removed your bandages?" he noted appreciatively, glancing at my forehead.

"Mostly," I agreed, fingering the broad, smooth Band-Aid over my brow.

The doctor had ordered me only to wear the thick cotton bandages until the stitches quit seeping, and this morning the bandage I had applied last night was dry and clean. The stitches had looked straighter and more orderly in the bathroom mirror too now that the swelling had gone down.

"Excellent." Klaus selected a warm roll from the basket in the middle of the table. "Frau Werner telephoned us this morning to talk about your friend."

My internal ruminations about the probable size and severity of a permanent forehead scar evaporated instantly. "What? Why?"

Greta clucked at our continued use of English but with less conviction than usual. Klaus buttered his roll unperturbedly. "She has located a…" He glanced up, frowning. "*Japanischen Übersetzer?*"

"Japanese translator," I supplied. "Coming to St. Goar? When?"

Klaus shrugged, now slathering his buttered roll with goose liver pâté. "Frau Werner only asked me to tell you a translator is coming. I think she is feeling the guilt because you have no service job."

"It's okay," I said hollowly. What would Shin reveal when the translator finally spoke to her? That someone had beaten her up and then someone else—a dumb gangly kid from the United States—had assaulted her in a darkened bakery entrance?

"You will tell your friend the translator is coming?" Klaus asked.

I shook my head. "She doesn't know enough German or English for me to tell her anything. That's why they need the translator."

"*Ja, ja, natürlich,*" Klaus agreed, frowning. "Yet you visited her all day yesterday. What did you do together if you could not speak?"

"We just walked around mostly. She was probably bored. I don't think I'll visit her again today."

"What?" Autumn said from behind me. The word snapped through the kitchen like shattering ice.

"*Ach so! Und hier kommt meine schöne Tochter,*" Klaus greeted her, beaming.

"*Guten Morgen, Vati,*" she said pleasantly.

Klaus's tiny eyes widened merrily at her use of the endearment *Vati*. He turned triumphantly to his wife, "*Siehst du, Gretelchen? Das Mädchen lernt es noch.*"

Autumn weaved behind my chair and sat down in her customary spot next to me and across from Klaus.

"Look…" I began.

"Later," she said curtly. She spent breakfast conversing airily in truly atrocious German with Klaus and Greta, both of whom obviously appreciated her efforts. Greta kissed her twice on each cheek when she stood up to leave for the greenhouse.

"Want to walk me partway, Leon?" she asked casually. I had an idea I shouldn't turn her down.

I thanked Greta for breakfast, pushed back from the table, and followed Autumn outside. She waited until we had reached street level to speak. When she did, her voice was surprisingly quiet. "I expected more of you, Leon."

I braced myself. I had earned this tongue lashing, even if did come from a girl who had made a fortune selling her body on the internet.

"I know your dad is a pastor and everything, and I know you take all the Mennonite peacemaking stuff seriously, but to cut Shin off like this…we can only guess what terrible things have happened to her." She sighed. "Maybe I shouldn't have said anything to you this morning."

"What are you talking about?"

"I heard you telling Klaus you weren't going to see Shin again. I know violence is like the big no-no for Mennonites, but I still wouldn't have thought your I'll-help-anyone attitude would fall apart the moment—"

"Wait, you think I'm avoiding Shin because she attacked Hat?"

She watched me warily. "What else could make you abandon

her after you practically killed yourself dragging her to the hospital the other day?"

Unexpected and unwelcome, a confession was rising in my throat like some oozing monster clawing its way out of a sewer pipe. "Something else happened last night."

"Something else," Autumn repeated. "Because last night wasn't weird enough already."

So I explained what had happened after Shin and I had left the pizzeria—the loud group of guys that had startled us into hiding in a bakery doorway, the way Shin had started crying, and finally how I had cataclysmically misjudged the situation and kissed her.

"And then what happened?" Autumn asked tensely.

"Then," I finished miserably, "I took her home."

Autumn looked very troubled. She seemed to be waiting for something. "That's it?"

"I don't know, she thanked me for some reason. She said *arigato* and everything, so I know I understood her. But I think she was just trying to make me feel better. Not that I should feel better. I guess I'm not such a safe guy to be around after all, am I?"

Autumn's hands rose dangerously to her hips. "God, you're pathetic sometimes."

I recoiled. It was the harshest thing anyone had ever said to me. And yet she didn't sound angry. I didn't have the slightest idea how to respond, so I clenched my jaw and kept silent.

Autumn made her annoyed *tch!* sound and grabbed the sides of my head. It felt very different than the way Shin had done it last night.

"I'm only going to tell you this once because even that's one time too many: snap the hell out of it. What you did last night was not cool but it wasn't evil either. You misread the moment and acted on some seriously overcharged emotions."

I tried to free myself. She clamped on even tighter.

"If you really want to wreck things with Shin then go ahead and ignore her. Keep up this self-indulgent pouting. If you want to do the right thing, grow up, be a man, and learn from your mistake."

"It's not like Shin needs any more help from me," I argued, the words sounding pouty indeed with my lips pooched out from Autumn's grip. "Frau Werner's got a translator coming in."

Autumn leaned up so that our noses nearly touched. Her breath, tangy-sweet from the strawberry jam she'd eaten with breakfast, puffed against my lips. "I've never met anyone as brave or selfless as you are when it comes to helping other people. So it's time to stop being such a pussy, and let yourself realize that you're the one who needs help right now."

She let go of my face, spun on her heel, and resumed her easy pace up the sidewalk as if nothing had happened. By the time I could even guess at what she'd meant, I had to run to catch up.

Autumn maintained an amiable silence until we reached the *Marktplatz*. Despite the troubled buzzing of my brain, I couldn't help but register how different she was than other girls at school, church, or in my family. I had never met anyone who could deliver a dressing down like that without holding some passive-aggressive grudge for the next few hours if not days, weeks, or years.

On the corner where we would part ways, Autumn toward work and I to the Hotel Schwarzer Bär—because there was no doubt I would visit Shin again today no matter how difficult the prospect might seem at the moment—she smiled bracingly and squeezed my shoulders. "You're going to be better now, right?"

"Yeah," I said, shrugging. Then, more confidently, "Yes. I feel better."

"I didn't say anything about feeling better," she corrected, amused. "I said you're going to *be* better.

"Now," she continued, suddenly all business. "You guys should go up to that old castle this morning. Riffles or whatever."

"Rheinfels? Why?"

She nodded. "Shin stared at it from her hotel room window all afternoon yesterday."

"Didn't you want to go there too?" I asked. "You've been talking about it since our first day here."

"Course," she said, pulling her guidebook out of her backpack and handing it to me. "But I want you to go first so you can learn all the boring history stuff and tell me the good parts when you and I go together later."

I accepted the book, thinking again of Autumn's emotions and the Space Mountain rollercoaster at Disneyland. "You're sure you're not mad at me?" I asked before I could stop myself.

A new emotion crossed her face. It took me a few seconds to identify; I had never seen Autumn look unsure about anything before.

"I *was* mad," she said slowly. "But I think I was mad *for* you instead of *at* you. You're a beautiful and righteously messed up person, Leon." She stood on tiptoe and planted a swift kiss on my cheek. It was nothing like the kiss Greta had given me when I'd left the house. "Have fun at the castle."

She set off across the street toward the greenhouse, reshouldering her bag as she went. My cheek tingled and burned where she'd kissed me. I thought again of my mother's warning that girls like Autumn Springer only know one way to interact with boys. Yet Autumn's kiss just now had been more sisterly than sexual, hadn't it?

Does a sister's kiss tingle like that? asked a small voice in my head.

But that was ridiculous. Autumn knew how I felt about Shin. She obviously wasn't trying to compete. I mean, if she liked me why would she insist I take Shin up to the castle today?

My palms were sweating against the glossy cover of Autumn's guidebook. I wiped them on my shorts and headed across the *Marktplatz*. The man with the heavy steel-colored eyebrows glanced up as I entered the lobby of the Hotel Schwarzer Bär.

"You come to visit your friend?" he said brightly. His eyebrows rose and quivered like the whiskers of a curious rodent.

I nodded and he pointed up the small staircase. With each step my heart seemed to jump upward too until it sat drumming in my throat as I reached the top landing. If Shin had spoken either English or German I could at least have worried about what I would say when she opened the door, but my Japanese vocabulary of "hello" and "thank you" wouldn't exactly rebuild any bridges.

Still unused to knocking on doors with my fists, I thumped a few times with my elbow, feeling the old dull ache ring through my wrist and hand like the toll of some grim bell.

The door creaked open almost right away as if Shin had been expecting a visitor. She still wore the pink *Kein Problem!* t-shirt and tan capris and I realized they were basically the only clothes she owned. Would she think I was even weirder if I tried to buy her more?

"Good morning."

"Hi," Shin said with a little bow.

I blinked. Had Autumn taught her that word? "Um, hi. Did you sleep good? Not that you can answer. Anyway, Frau Werner found a translator for you but I don't know when they'll actually get here. So I thought—well, actually it was Autumn's idea but I agreed…"

She seemed be watching me more cautiously than normal, possibly due more to my babbling than fear that I would try to take advantage of her again.

I took a deep breath. "I'm sorry about last night. I promise I won't do anything like that again without your permission. Which you can't really give, so let's just say no more monkey business and we can go back to being friends. Cool?"

She cocked her head slightly to one side, dark eyes wide and knowing. Had Autumn also taught her that look?

I cleared my throat. "I would like to take you to Burg Rheinfels today. It's the big castle up on the…hang on."

I thumbed clumsily through the guidebook, almost dropping

it at one point. My hands certainly felt better now than they had when I'd first come to St. Goar but that old feeling of steel wool packed into my knuckles was returning.

I gave up on the book and simply pointed out the window. "Autumn says you were really enamored with that big castle yesterday." I pointed to Shin, then at myself, then back through the window. "You want to go with me up there?"

But her attention was focused on my hands, a familiar little frown creasing her forehead.

"It's okay," I said quickly. "My own fault for playing that stupid game yesterday. I still feel better than I have in a long time." I moved toward the door.

"*Aniyo,*" Shin said sternly. Now she was the one pointing, to the bed rather than out the window. "*Kumbang gatta olkkeyo.*"

She disappeared into the restroom and came back a moment later with the lacquered box of needles in her hand. Her thin eyebrows rose when she saw I hadn't moved. She pointed to the bed again. "*Kogi.*" Her meaning could not have been clearer. I sat down on the edge of the bed as instructed.

4

Fifteen minutes later I found myself back outside on the cobblestone pavilion of the *Marktplatz,* Shin at my side. My hands felt cool and vaguely—wonderfully—hollow. The packed steel wool sensation had fled from Shin's needles like a besieging army under a barrage from skilled archers. I found myself wriggling my fingers every few seconds just to make sure they were still attached. The day seemed awfully fine all of a sudden.

"Autumn's right, isn't she?" I said, grinning. "Right again, I should say. I'd been thinking of her as emotionally unstable and hard to read but *I'm* the one, not her. I barely recognize myself since I came here. One minute I'm over the moon about something and the next I'm drowning in my own misery."

Shin walked silently beside me as had become our custom, seeming content to let me go on. Which was good, because I couldn't shut up. She was like a living diary that soaked up my ramblings without judgment. Was this what Autumn had meant when she'd said I needed help?

The quickest route to Rheinfels Castle took us down the same pedestrian-only *Fußgängerzone* where we had walked yesterday morning from the hospital and once in the evening from the pizza place. Shin suddenly tugged my arm and pointed up the street. "*Poseyo! Paegop'ayo?*"

For one horrified moment, I thought she was pointing at the bakery entrance half a block away where I had almost wrecked everything last night. But when I leaned down and followed her line of sight more closely I understood she was pointing to a second bakery, across the street and farther down than the first one.

"Oh yeah, that's where we got those pretzels. There must be more bakeries in Germany than there are Starbucks in the States. So you're hungry?" She grinned so eagerly that I couldn't help laughing. "Did Autumn and I forget to tell you about breakfast at your hotel? Okay, pretzels it is."

But as soon as we stepped inside I wished we'd gone to the other bakery, bad memories or no. Hat was standing at the counter wearing dark sunglasses. Shin went rigid beside me and I instinctively grabbed her hand.

A woman behind the counter folded the top of a paper bag and passed it to Hat. "*Einen Euro fünfzig bitte.*"

Hat winced at the woman's voice as if she were clashing cymbals next to his ears. He muttered, "*Danke,*" and dumped a few coins onto one of the many little countertop money trays that to Germans seemed to prefer over exchanging money directly by hand. He turned toward the door, the bag in his hand already blooming with grease spots from the treat within. It was too late for Shin and me to duck back out without being seen. How angry had he been last night when he'd come around? Could he have complained to Frau Werner already this morning? I squeezed Shin's hand and waited for the explosion.

Hat's eyebrows rose behind his sunglasses when he saw us. "What's up?" he said. "You guys look as bad as I feel, like some mafia dude shoved your faces into a wood chipper. No offense."

Shin's black eyes flicked up to mine, confusion and worry flashing in them like distant lightning.

Hat tapped his sunglasses, apparently under the impression that they were the source of our concern. "I'm wearing these because I went on a bender last night at this pizza joint. She was there," he added, indicating Shin. "I remember ordering a couple beers and then waking up on the ground. Autumn said I fell out of my chair and cracked my skull. I feel like there's a pissed off dwarf trying to bang his way out of my head with a pickaxe."

He bent his elbow and rolled his shoulder experimentally, wincing. "I must have hit my funny bone or something too. My arm aches like a hooker."

His forearm showed a long series of scrapes like road rash. Had he noticed that the "scrape" by his elbow was actually a little cluster of pinpricks?

"Uh," I licked my lips, "sorry, man. Is there anything we can do for you?"

"Nah. Some chick in the drugstore down the street gave me a box of aspirin or whatever. Did you know that headache in German is *Kapschmutzen?*" he added knowledgeably.

The word was actually *Kopfschmerzen,* but I didn't bother to correct him. "Hey, at least you learned some new vocab, right?"

"Yeah right. Anyway I need to bury this headache before I hit the soccer pitch. Check you later."

"Later," I echoed, stepping aside with Shin to let him pass. When he had disappeared into the pedestrian traffic on the *Fußgängerzone* I let out a long breath. "So that just happened."

Shin frowned up at me, still confused but looking less worried now.

"He doesn't remember," I explained happily. To the woman behind the counter, I said, *"Zwei Bretzeln, bitte."*

Back outside, the sun seemed to have climbed halfway up the

sky in the last five minutes and the temperature seemed to have risen another ten degrees. It was shaping up to be a real scorcher. Even so, my pretzel was hot enough to steam when I tore away the first bite. Shin nibbled fretfully at her own, clutching it close to her chest in both hands as if taking warmth from it. I wondered fleetingly if putting my arm around her shoulders would make her feel better or worse.

"Maybe you can teach me some Japanese," I suggested. "Like, I know *konnichiwa* means hello. So how would I say, 'My name is Leon'?"

Shin glanced up in recognition when I said *konnichiwa* but the familiar word didn't make her any happier. Her lips were starting to press together the way they had last night before she'd started crying.

"That's okay," I said quickly. "You don't have to teach me anything."

We walked in heavy silence for another block, during which I finished the rest of my pretzel and Shin continued to take little mouse bites from hers. The *Fußgängerzone* terminated at a curving, steeply slanted motorway that led from town up to the castle. Heavy traffic buzzed past in both directions.

Shin and I stood side by side, waiting for an opening. When one finally appeared I took her hand again and stepped into the street. That empty, peaceful feeling in my hands persisted even with our fingers interlaced and twisting as we jogged across the street and leapt up onto the opposite sidewalk.

"You know, I'm starting to think you were some kind of doctor or nurse in Japan," I told her. "Whatever Frau Werner thinks, I doubt they teach prostitutes how to perform acu—"

A sharp screech of car brakes made us both nearly jump out of our shoes. A short way up the hill to our left a whole line of cars was braking hard, tail lights glaring and blue smoke drifting up from locked tires. I tensed, anticipating a loud crunch of metal that never came. A few drivers honked their horns in irritation but there didn't seem to have been a wreck.

"A cat probably ran out in front of somebody," I said. "Anyway, what were we talking about?"

But Shin was staring transfixed up the street toward the stopped cars. She suddenly squeezed my hand so hard that I could hear my knuckles grind together. My knees buckled with the agony of it. Hot tears gushed instantly from my eyes.

Then, just as quickly as it had come, the pressure was gone. I heard Shin's small feet pounding down the sidewalk in the opposite direction from the traffic jam. She was shouting something that might have been a cry for help or meaningless, terrified babble.

Before I could straighten up or call out to her, a meaty forearm as thick as my own leg thudded into my chest and I sprawled backward onto the sidewalk. All of the air gusted from my lungs with a single, quiet "*Hoo!*"

I struggled to sit up and failed. Between the screaming fire my left hand had become and the fact that I seemed to be trying to breathe in a vacuum, the best I could do was lift my head off the sidewalk in time to see an impossibly muscular bald man the size of a polar bear stride briskly past where I lay, Shin thrown over his shoulder. She was kicking furiously and tearing at his back with her fingernails. I could see her trying to bite into his shoulder, but either his shirt was too thick or she was being jostled too much to do any real damage.

She looked down at me, shining black hair bouncing against her cheeks, eyes so wide they seemed to fill the whole top half of her face, and screamed, "Ree-yong! *Dowa jwoyo! Tasukete!*"

"*Halt die Fresse,*" the man barked impassively over his shoulder.

With an effort I would have believed impossible a second ago, I rocked forward into a sitting position.

"Ree-yong!" Shin wailed again.

But her voice was too quiet, already too far away. I funneled every shred of strength I possessed into my legs and finally, shaking, regained my feet.

More shouts. Several heads were poking out of car windows, some gesturing for the muscular man to halt—the man who had attacked Autumn in the bar, the man who had slashed my forehead. But no one dared confront him directly. He still wasn't even running, though he certainly could have. Shin must have weighed about as much as a cotton swab to him.

I staggered forward, holding my belly. Somewhere up ahead, over the crest of a small hill in the road, a car door slammed, cutting off Shin's desperate cries. Another squeal of tires, a roar of an engine, and Shin was gone.

5

"Wer waren die beiden?"
"Was ist passiert?"
"Ist das Mädchen entführt worden?"

I caught snatches of these same questions over and over through the gridlocked street as I pelted, clutching my gut, toward the cloud of dust and exhaust still swirling at the hilltop where Shin had been kidnapped. Some of the motorists only poked their heads curiously out of their windows, while a braver few had actually stepped out of their vehicles and now peered over the doors as if ready to duck behind them at the first sign of danger. Thankfully, I also glimpsed a number of cell phones glinting in the sunlight.

Please be calling the police, I thought desperately. I would gladly have borrowed one of their phones to do just that, but slippery bolts of panic were stabbing through my brain and I doubted my German would be up to a detailed telephone conversation with a police officer at the moment.

"*Junge!*" another voice called.

I ignored this one as well. I didn't stop running until I'd reached the top of the rise. Drivers in the oncoming lane were already honking for the line to get moving. It seemed impossible that they hadn't seen Shin getting shoved into that guy's car.

"*Junge!*" the same voice insisted, now panting close behind me. "*Bleib stehen.*"

A strong hand gripped my bicep and I turned to find the flushed, square-jawed face of a middle-aged German woman staring back up at me.

"Let me go." My voice rasped distantly in my ears as if from an old, busted radio. "*Lass mich frei,*" I added, neither knowing nor caring whether this was the correct translation.

The woman held my arm fast, but her voice was gentle, motherly. "*Ist sie deine Freundin?*"

I ignored her, attempting to slow my breathing. A plan was already forming in my head. The other day Autumn had told me the bartender she'd met our first night here had recognized the bodybuilder. Said the guy might even have caused some trouble before. Maybe the bartender would know his name. And if the police had a name, they could also find an address.

Assuming he takes her back to his house instead of leaving her for dead in another field.

"Shut up," I snarled.

"*Was sagst du denn?*" the motherly woman asked, alarmed.

"*Sie ist meine Frau,*" I lied mechanically. Would the woman believe I was old enough to be married? "*Können Sie bitte die Polizei anrufen?*"

Whether she believed me or not, she pulled a cell phone from her purse and dialed three numbers before holding the phone to her ear. I recalled from German class that Germany's version of 911 was something like 110 or 112. I couldn't remember exactly, and it didn't matter. I thanked the woman and immediately started toward downtown.

"*Warte,*" she called after me.

But I couldn't wait. I had to speak to the bartender. The pub was located this side of downtown and I had to rediscover the correct alley without Autumn's voice to guide—

"Leon! There you are."

I spun around. Autumn was trotting toward me from one of the many side streets in this part of town, smiling and waving.

"I don't think I'm going to get in a full day's work all summer," she said happily, halting in front of me. "Frau Werner just showed up at the greenhouse and asked me to...what's the matter? Why didn't you pick up Shin?"

To my horror, tears suddenly welled in my eyes. "Shin's been kidnapped."

There was a moment's heavy silence, Autumn a yellow and pink blur in my vision.

"You mean she wasn't in her room? Maybe she went out for breakfast."

I steadied myself. "We were walking toward the castle. That big muscle guy from the bar jumped out of his car, pushed me down, and carried Shin away. I think a few people have already called the police but I doubt anyone knows who the guy is. I was just about to go ask your bartender friend if he could tell the police a name. Maybe they can find him before..." But there was no good way to end that sentence. "Anyway, I need to hurry."

I started off toward downtown again but Autumn caught my arm. "Oh my God, Leon. That guy's arms—remember how they were covered in all those little red dots in the bar?"

I did remember. The red dots had looked like needle tracks, which I supposed now they were. And there had been a little cluster of marks near his elbow, very similar to the ones currently decorating Hat's arm.

I shook my head so violently that sweat flew from the ends of my hair. "We can worry about this later. Shin's in trouble right now and we have to get her back."

"You're right." She took a breath. "Of course you're right. But let me do it."

"Do what?"

"Well, I came to find you because Frau Werner wants to see you this morning at ten o'clock in her office. You should just have enough time to get there if you leave now. So I'll go talk to the bartender—"

I turned my back on her and started walking again. She didn't understand. She hadn't seen or heard Shin being stuffed into that car. Whatever Frau Werner wanted to say could wait. I had made it halfway down the block by the time Autumn caught my arm again.

I rounded on her. "You were the one telling me not to abandon Shin. Now you want me to stroll over to Frau Werner's office like nothing happened and let Shin get murdered by that Neanderthal?"

I expected her to get up in my face and tell me to cool it. I welcomed the argument. I was so sick of her acting like she knew how I should behave in any given situation. So sick of her thinking she was the strong, sensible one and I was an ignorant child. Nothing could have prepared me for the tenderness with which she stepped into me, arms circling my waist, and laid her head on my shoulder.

"Of course I don't want that." Her breath puffed against my neck. It still smelled like strawberries. "I'm terrified for her, Leon. I'm so sorry all these things have happened."

It was as if her hug, though gentle, had squeezed all the moisture in my body up to my eyes. I suddenly convulsed against her as if strapped to an electric generator, unable even to lift my arms to reciprocate the hug.

"We'll find her," Autumn vowed. Her lips fluttered against my neck like flower petals in a breeze.

I cleared my throat and sniffed several times, trying to recover some control over myself. The sounds must have grossed her out but she continued to hold me.

"I dropped your guidebook," I said. "When that guy hit me. I forgot to pick it up."

She clung to me more tightly. "It doesn't matter."

"I'll go see Frau Werner," I said. "Tell her what happened. The more people know what happened, the sooner…"

"The sooner we'll get her back," Autumn finished. She stepped away at last, hands still on my hips as if to steady me from falling. Her eyes were pink and shiny, but her cheeks were dry. Only I had actually cried.

"What will you do when you get back from the church?" she asked.

"Probably go to the nearest police station and wait for news. They'll be the most up to date."

"Will you wait for me at the *Marktplatz* so we can go together? I want to be with you."

I sniffed again. "I'm okay."

She gave a strangled laugh. "Well bully for you. I'm not okay in the slightest."

"I'll wait," I promised. "Just hurry."

6

The low, dark hallway outside Frau Werner's office door smelled of coffee and cinnamon. At first I thought she might have another little dessert party planned for me and I doubted my uneasy stomach could handle even a sip of coffee right now. But as she waved me into the room, she swept crumbs from a small saucer into her wastebasket and threw back a small mug of coffee like a heavy drinker tossing a shot of whiskey. She grimaced with pleasure as she tucked the mug and saucer into a desk drawer.

"Good morning, Leon. Thank you for coming so quickly." Something about my demeanor must have worried her because her back straightened in sudden concern. "What has happened now? Has Ronald hurt himself again?"

"No, but—wait, what?" My brain had just caught the full import of what she'd said. She knew about Hat's injury last night but she seemed to think he had done it to himself. Even in my distress I had to hand it to Autumn. She knew how to spin a web of secrets.

"Perhaps you did not hear of it," Frau Werner said tersely.

"Ronald had an unfortunate accident involving alcohol at a local restaurant."

"Ah," I said awkwardly. "No, I saw him this morning in a bakery. He seems fine. But something much more serious happened."

I described Shin's kidnapping in as much detail as I could remember, beginning after we had left Hat in the bakery, and ending with Autumn's promise to go speak with the bartender in the hope of learning the kidnapper's identity. For an event that had consumed my entire life in the last fifteen minutes or so, it took a surprisingly short time to tell.

Frau Werner sat even straighter in her chair now, her long face pale and rigid inside its helmet of hair. "You are sure it was the same man who attacked you and Autumn in the Kneipe?"

"Yes," I said firmly. "You couldn't mistake this guy for anyone else. He's massive."

"And you cannot guess what interest he had in your friend? The reason he wanted to take her?"

I frowned. "I don't...Why does that matter? Shin is with him right now, and we've seen how he treats women. He might have killed Autumn if I hadn't stepped between them."

Frau Werner surveyed me across her desk without responding. This wordless appraisal simultaneously made me want to bellow defiant things at her and hide behind my chair but I made myself stare right back at her. I don't know how long it continued—probably only a few seconds—before the telephone on her desk jangled loudly, making me jump. Frau Werner hardly blinked as she reached over and lifted the receiver.

"Good morning, Anna Werner speaking."

I readjusted myself in the chair, nerves still humming, but glad that the call had at least distracted her from staring me.

"Ah, thank you for calling. I know the rates can be expensive... Yes, it is the correct time. He is right here. One moment."

And then she was holding out the telephone handset across her desk toward me. I stared at it, only now realizing how odd it was that Frau Werner had answered the call in English.

"I asked your mother to call my office this morning to speak with you," she said.

I gaped at her. "Why would…No. I can talk to my mother later. Shin—"

"You have already told me that at least one person called the police and Autumn is attempting to learn the kidnapper's name," Frau Werner persisted, holding the phone out doggedly over her desk. "And I will make further inquiries by cell phone while you speak to your mother. This call is costing her a great deal of money."

Mom's voice crackled uncertainly from the earpiece in Frau Werner's hand. "Leon? Hello?"

I snatched the phone from Frau Werner with an ill-tempered glare. "Hey, Mom."

"Oh, there you are," she said, her tone falsely bright. How much had Frau Werner told her? "I guess you got to Germany all right?"

"I got here," I agreed. "I meant to email but a lot has happened."

Frau Werner gave me a quick nod that was evidently supposed to be encouraging but looked to me more like the sort of gesture a general might make to a soldier he was sending out on a suicide mission. She rose and left the room, presumably to make her promised inquiries, whatever those might be.

"How has the weather been?" Mom attempted bravely.

"Mom, I'm sorry, but my friend is in trouble and I don't really have time to explain."

She might have sighed, or it could have been a soft wash of static over the line. "That Springer girl? I just knew she would make—"

"No, Autumn is fine. She's been great, in fact. She's kept me company while Frau Werner looks for a service assignment for me. She even helped me when my hands were really bad the first morning here."

A worried silence greeted this news. It almost seemed like Mom wanted Autumn to be a problem.

"She's been great," I repeated vindictively.

The silence stretched. I could almost hear Mom's fretful internal monologue, something along the lines of: *What's happened to my sweet little boy?* Or likelier still: *What has that awful girl done to him?*

"Why did Frau Werner ask you to call me?" I asked. My voice shook, whether out of panic or fury I couldn't tell.

"She said you seemed very upset with your experience so far, and she thought you might be getting homesick. It happens to anyone the first time they leave home."

"Homesick?" I actually laughed. It was a sarcastic, unpleasant sound. "At least she caught on that I'm upset. The reason why is no big mystery, is it? I worked all year to raise money for a service trip only to get here and find out no one wants a crippled volunteer. So I found my own service project and Frau Werner has done nothing but discourage me. So to be honest, with all the disappointment and discouragement flying around I haven't found time to miss home."

"You can just stop that right now," Mom said, her voice hoarse and shocked. "Whatever you've been through, there is no excuse for speaking to me that way."

I blinked. What *had* happened to me? I'd never said such ugly things to her in my life. "I'm sorry."

"I forgive you," she said rather stiffly. "I can tell you are hurting and I hope you will let me help."

"You can't do anything. I know you want to," I added, striving not to sound bitter or sarcastic.

"You said your friend was in trouble," Mom pressed on. "Is it that Springer g—Is it Autumn?" she amended.

"No, Autumn is fine." And suddenly, even though it was the very last thing I wanted to do, I found myself explaining all about

Shin to my mother—how Autumn and I had carried her, injured and starving, to the hospital; how I'd learned she had been abused by someone in St. Goar; how Frau Werner and the Holzes refused to give her a place to stay and Autumn had bought a hotel with her own money; how, in other words, Shin had become my service project.

"And this morning," I finished, "a man jumped out of his car, attacked me, and kidnapped her. I'm sure it was the same guy who beat her up the first time. He could be doing anything to her right now."

I carefully left out any mention of Autumn's altercation with Shin's kidnapper, as well as the fact that I had allowed Shin to use acupuncture on my hands. I guessed the latter would actually worry Mom more than the former. Unitarian mantras aside, she had little tolerance for unorthodox—which to her meant anything not generally accepted by Midwestern middle-class Mennonites— ideas or behaviors.

She didn't say a word the whole time I spoke. I thought she must be digesting it all, struggling to come up with some way to help or at least something to say to make me feel better.

"We're bringing you home," she said at last.

I almost dropped the phone. "What?"

"Leon, what if that man comes looking for you next? You aren't old enough to understand what a dangerous situation you've put yourself in. You don't really know anything about that girl or her relationship with the man you think kidnapped her. She could be a criminal and he could be a police officer who is supposed to catch her."

"Mom, that's not—"

"You don't know!" Mom repeated hysterically. "Leon, I want you to promise you won't go looking for her before we can buy you a plane ticket home."

"I'm not coming home," I said indignantly. "I've got—"

"Leon!" she shrieked, totally losing control now. "Your father and I will fly to Germany to pick you up ourselves if that's what it takes. We should never have let you go. You're too fragile to be on your own in a foreign—"

I slammed the phone down onto its cradle and backed away, irrationally terrified that Mom's voice would start spitting and hissing out of it like an angry snake even though the connection had been severed. My back collided against the office door and I spun around, scrabbling at the knob. I had to get out of here.

But the knob twisted under my fingers and Frau Werner pushed the door open from the other side, a satisfied expression on her face. "*Ach,* Leon, you have already finished speaking with your mother?"

I nodded, not trusting myself to speak. Mom could call back any second.

"Very good. You will be pleased to hear that the police have already found your friend."

"Really? How? Is she all right? Where is she?"

"Too many people witnessed her capture for the kidnapper to get very far. They have both been taken to the *Polizeiinspektion* across the river in Werlau. There is no station here in St. Goar," Frau Werner explained. "Your friend did not seem to have any new injuries. A medical worker has been summoned to make certain."

"And the kidnapper?"

"He is giving a statement. It seems he has been arrested for violent behavior before."

I ran shaking fingers across the sharp stubble of my stitches. "No kidding. The police told you all that?"

"I maintain a close relationship with the police in each of the regions where I work, as I explained to you earlier."

Relief swept through me like healing wind. Shin was alive. The man hadn't been able to hurt her again. Furthermore, I was beginning to see why the conversation with my mother had gone so very wrong. After checking in on Shin I should buy one of those pre-paid telephone cards and call her back from a payphone, smooth everything over.

Frau Werner broke into these happy thoughts, still looking rather grim. "The police may want to speak with you about what you saw this morning."

"I'll tell them everything," I said at once. "I've got nothing to hide."

She hesitated. "Also, in light of what happened, the Japanese translator will make a special trip to Werlau today. He may be in town within the hour."

"That's great!" I beamed at her. This meeting was turning into a real blizzard of good news. "Can I visit Shin now?"

The telephone on her desk rang again. This time I jumped so violently that had I been sitting down I would have fallen out of my chair.

"It is only the telephone, Leon," Frau Werner said. "You are a very tense boy."

"Yeah, I'll work on that," I said, edging toward the door. "I'm going to visit Shin now, okay? You said she's in Werlau? Across the river?"

Her hand hovered over the telephone, which seemed to ring more violently in response to the delay. "Yes. You can find it on your own?"

"No problem."

And then the telephone was in her hand, rising to her ear. Abandoning all subtlety, I leapt into the hallway and broke into a dead run. I just barely heard her voice drift down the hallway—"*Hallo, ich bin's,*"—before I crashed through the heavy wooden church doors into the hot summer morning.

7

I ran until I'd put at least three blocks between myself and the church, and even then I maintained a shuffling jog. That phone call must have been my mother again. Would Frau Werner be able to talk her down, or would the two women agree that I should return home? They certainly seemed to share a deep distrust in my relationship with Shin.

I forced these unpleasant thoughts down. Let them simmer in the depths of my mind for the moment. More important was the fact that the police had Shin's attacker in custody now, and I could think of no better atonement for my actions last night than to give testimony that would keep him there.

The *Marktplatz* was already buzzing with its usual late morning contingent of tourists and harried looking Germans out for their daily errands. Would Autumn be here yet? Would I even be able to find her in this crowd?

But those questions were answered for me almost immediately. Autumn, Elise, and Bernie were parked at one of the heavy iron tables on the nearest edge of the plaza. As I started toward them, the Italian waiter who had gotten into that scrap with Hat yesterday delivered three giant bowls and three glasses of mineral water to their table. He didn't look any friendlier today but at least he wasn't shouting. I arrived at the table just as he set the last bowl—full of what appeared to be spaghetti covered in whipped cream—in front of Bernie.

"*Vielen Dank, guter Mann,*" Bernie said gamely. He flipped a Euro coin onto the waiter's now empty tray. Noticing me he added, "There he is, just in time to mooch off the rest of us."

The waiter glared down at the coin on his tray, then up at me as if blaming me for my friends' behavior. "*Für Sie?*" he said gruffly.

Caught off guard, I ordered a scoop of hazelnut ice cream and sat down. "What are you guys doing here?" But before they could answer I stood up again. "What am I doing here? Sorry, I need to go. I'll explain later."

I flung a few Euro coins on the table to pay for the hazelnut ice cream I didn't have time to eat.

Autumn seized my wrist. "The boat to Werlau doesn't leave for another forty-five minutes. Have a seat. Wait for your ice cream."

"How did you—" I began, but there were at least three important questions that started with those words and I couldn't decide on any one of them.

"The bartender knew the bodybuilder guy's name right away," Autumn explained. "Get this: he's actually famous. I told you the other day I thought the cops had recognized him."

"Famous?"

"He does those moronic Strongest Man in the World competitions on TV."

I shook my head. "We don't get cable."

Bernie piped up, "It's a tournament where a bunch of guys with no necks take turns lifting motorcycles and giant stone balls to see which of them can grunt the hardest without pooping himself. My older brothers used to watch it all the time."

"Anyway," said Autumn with a sideways glance at Bernie, "the bartender called the cops as soon as I told him what happened, but they'd already picked up that guy and Shin. The bartender told me they must be in Werlau, across the river, because they have the only police station for miles."

Autumn pulled a stack of four credit-card sized tickets from her pocket and handed me one. It was printed with today's date and the words *St. Goar—Werlau Fähre Tagespass.*

"With these we can go back and forth across the river," she said. "All of us, as many times as we want. We're—we all want to know that Shin is okay."

She sort of twitched in her seat as if she wanted to stand up but thought better of it. I recalled suddenly how she had hugged me earlier. Neither of us moved or spoke, but something must have passed between us because Elise and Bernie exchanged embarrassed glances. Blushing, I slid the ferry ticket carefully into my pocket alongside the scrap of paper with Shin's name on it and finally sat down again. "What about you two? You don't have any reason to go with us."

"Autumn stopped by the greenhouse on her way to the docks to buy the tickets," Elise explained in the same tone of earnest concern she'd used when asking about my arthritis at the church mixer. Despite the enormous square movie star sunglasses she was wearing today, it was easy to imagine her equally enormous eyes behind them, wide and dark and moist with concern. "She thought you wouldn't mind some extra company."

"And then I saw these ladies sitting here while I was on my morning constitutional," Bernie said with his bizarre dignity. "The daycare where I was supposed to start working today is closed until Monday because all the kids are home yarfing with the flu."

"Gross," said Elise.

"That's very cool of you guys," I said thickly. "I've had kind of a lousy day. Maybe a few of them," I added, fingering my stitches again.

"Hey, we also got to know your friend a little bit last night," Bernie said reassuringly. "She seemed cool. Maybe a little stabby."

Elise choked and spluttered on her mineral water, most of which ran foaming down the front of her shirt. Autumn stared at Bernie as though she were considering mashing her ice cream into his face.

Bernie acknowledged neither reaction. He scooped up a generous spoonful of "spaghetti"—which I saw now was not spaghetti at all but vanilla ice cream sculpted to look like noodles covered in a red fruit topping—and crammed it into his mouth. Without swallowing, he smiled grotesquely, ice cream and red sauce oozing through his teeth onto his chin, and said, "Mmm, pa-sketti!"

"What the hell, Bernie?" said Autumn, grinning in spite of herself.

I burst out laughing. I couldn't help it. Even Elise was fighting a smile. I felt some of the tension drain out of my shoulders. The girls seemed more relaxed too.

Bernie dabbed his chin without saying anything, looking supremely pleased with himself. When the waiter returned with my ice cream, Bernie dumped the soiled napkins on his tray. "Another round of serving tissues, my good man. My friends are absolute pigs."

We didn't see the waiter again. The next thirty minutes passed in animated, convivial conversation. More than once I was struck by the realization that, no matter how difficult the last few days had been, I already had more friends in St. Goar than I'd ever had in Iowa.

"Are you kidding?" Bernie was saying to Elise. "My parents made me come here. They offered me and my brothers a deal that if we did two years of voluntary service with MCC after high school they'd pay for our college."

"MCC?" Autumn interrupted.

"Mennonite Central Committee," I supplied automatically. "It's exactly what it sounds like."

Bernie nodded. "Anyway, my brothers like epitomize Kansas farm boys. You know—blond, square, and hairy. Straw bales on legs. They were perfectly happy to go build orphanages in Ecuador for two years and then come back to community college and major in cow-heaving or whatever. But I got a full scholarship to the Pre-Med program at KU. They don't accept many students and there's no guarantee I'd get in again next year."

He sighed theatrically. "Mom and Dad got all stern with me. They said I needed do some kind of service project this summer, get a taste of what it's like to help my fellow man so I could come home and make a more informed decision about the fall. Because medicine never helped anyone, right?"

Elise gave one of her amused snorts.

Bernie twirled his spoon fitfully in the pink dregs of his ice cream bowl. "So that's my deal. What are the rest of you mugs in for?"

"Excess of money," said Autumn brusquely. "My dad worried I'd blow my fortune on designer handbags and Chihuahuas, so he made me come here."

Bernie was the only one who laughed.

"My dad cheated on my mom last year," Elise said, almost too softly to hear. "They're still together but it's awful. I couldn't wait until September to get out of the house."

No one laughed this time. For once Bernie seemed to have nothing to say.

"I shouldn't have told you that, I'm sorry. It's not your problem," Elise said, blushing so deeply that color had crept above her sunglasses into her hairline.

Autumn gazed thoughtfully across the table at her. "We're all in good company, aren't we? Embarrassed by, and embarrassments to, our families. I'm starting to think that's just the human condition."

Elise gave her a watery smile.

"All except Leon, of course," Autumn said, reaching over to

163

clap my shoulder. "This guy would never do anything to upset his parents, right buddy?"

My mother's words echoed through my head: *We should never have let you go!*

Autumn tossed a crumpled napkin into her empty bowl and rose from the table. "Let's head for the docks. We want to be on that boat."

8

The motor of the double decker ferry rumbled loudly enough to make the steel boarding ramp vibrate under our feet. I followed the other three through the ferry's main cabin and up a flight of stairs to the upper deck, a broad arena of metal benches shimmering with heat. Elise eyed the benches doubtfully, tugging at the hem of her shorts as if worried they would not protect her thighs from getting burned.

Autumn walked to the stern, unfolded a map from her pocket, and spread it across the wide gunwale. Bernie and Elise each held down one side of it so it would not be ripped away on the draft blowing downriver. We all squinted down at it even though the town of Werlau was easily visible across the river.

"Looks like the police station is right on the riverbank, just a block or so from the dock," said Autumn.

Elise looked up and pointed at a low brown building, distinct only by virtue of being rather broader and squarer than the other low brown buildings around it. "Is that it?"

"Could be." Autumn refolded the map, a tricky job with the wind trying to snatch it out of her hands. "We'll just have to see when we get there."

The ferry shuddered under our feet as the engines kicked to full power. The floor tilted gently back. Directly below us greenish murk swirled around the propellers, which were otherwise invisible under the dirty water.

Off balance, Elise threw herself onto one of the benches and hissed at the sudden heat on the backs of her thighs. But she didn't stand up. Her cheeks were pale under her sunglasses. "Don't like boats," she said tightly.

Bernie, on the other hand, seemed to love boats. He clambered onto one of the many locked wooden boxes set against the gunwales, clutched the chrome railing that ran the whole perimeter of the deck, and turned his face happily into the wind.

"He looks like a dog sticking its face out a car window," Autumn laughed.

"My mom called me this morning," I said, taking care to speak too quietly for Bernie or Elise to overhear.

Her eyes widened. "Is that why Frau Werner wanted you?"

"Sure is."

"What did you talk about?"

I was sure Autumn already suspected that Mom thought the worst of her, but I saw no reason to go into detail about that part of our conversation. "I told her about Shin," I said simply.

"How did that go?"

I braced for an explosion. "She wants me to come home."

Threads of golden hair whipped around her unreadable eyes. There was no yelling, no explosion. "You can't," she said at last.

"I know. I'm planning to call her back after I've figured out how to convince her to let me stay."

The ferry had already traveled almost halfway across the river. Elise was still grasping the metal bench with white knuckles as if we were on a speedboat instead of a lumbering passenger ferry that rolled along at the pace of a brisk walk. Bernie remained equally motionless, perched on the box and leaning on the railing.

"I estimate we have about five more minutes," he called authoritatively over his shoulder. He sounded disappointed. "The river sure is narrow."

He wasn't far off. The four of us piled off the dock in Werlau a scant fifteen minutes after we had left port in St. Goar. The building Elise had pointed at earlier was indeed the police station. Low, broad, and painted a nondescript brown, it sat on the east side of a meandering road that followed the line of the river.

Bernie swept the door open and ushered the rest of us into the station lobby with a butler's flourish. Frau Werner was standing at the reception window, straight backed as a palace guard. Several paces to her right stood a high steel door that presumably led into the station itself. The only other feature in the lobby was a wooden display in which hundreds of faded maps and brochures drooped like wilted flowers.

Frau Werner's brows rose in mild surprise at the sight of Autumn, Bernie, and Elise piling into the small lobby behind me, but she nodded to them in greeting. I took it as an ill omen that she had taken the trouble to cross the river herself. Did that mean that Mom had called her back and demanded my return?

Autumn seemed to be thinking the same thing. She grabbed my hand, mercifully remembering not to squeeze it.

As usual, Frau Werner came right to the point. "Leon, it was inappropriate of you to cut off your conversation with your mother."

"I know, I panicked."

Her stern expression softened. "I spoke to her again after you left my office. She admitted that she had not been particularly calm either. I have convinced her to allow you to stay for the duration of your term."

"Are—are you serious? That's wonderful, thank you."

Now Frau Werner did smile, exposing broad, slightly uneven teeth. "I also accept some of the responsibility for your heightened stress over the last few days. I trust you will telephone your mother to apologize?"

"Yes," I said at once. "I was planning to call her after I leave here."

Frau Werner nodded, satisfied, and turned to the reception window. A pleasant looking man with graying hair and a crisp olive-green uniform was watching us politely from behind the glass. He must have been sitting there the whole time. He and Frau Werner shared a rapid but muted conversation after which he stood and marched purposefully away from his desk. A series of deep, grinding clicks echoed through the lobby and the steel door swung open. The man stuck his head into the lobby and gestured for us to enter, much like Bernie had done moments before.

"What, we can just go in?" Autumn asked. "All of us? Leon is the only one who saw what happened this morning."

"The police no longer need to ask Leon any questions. The man who attacked the girl—" She glanced at the officer holding the door. "—already confessed to the kidnapping, and we are waiting to verify his story with the translator."

"Really?" I said. "So the translator's already here too? Can I be with her during the interview?"

"Yes, I have already made that request and the police agreed," said Frau Werner. "Although I did not realize all of you would be coming. I am not certain whether—"

"It's okay, we'll wait out here," Autumn said. "Right guys?"

Bernie and Elise murmured their assent.

Frau Werner looked relieved. "Please go inside, Leon. Your friend is waiting."

9

The room behind the reception window consisted of perhaps twenty desks, behind most of which sat more uniformed men and women clacking out reports on desktop computers. This office area was much colder than the lobby, possibly to compensate for the fact that the uniforms had long sleeves and looked to be made of heavy wool.

Here and there along the perimeter of the room were more heavy steel doors and regular office doors with long, official looking names leading to other parts of the station. After attempting to puzzle out the nearest one, *Bundesgeschwindigkeitsbegrenzung u. Verkehrsmittel*, I gave up the rest as a bad job.

And anyway, I had just spotted Shin sitting in front of a vacant desk on the other side of the room. She looked pale and nervous and cold but otherwise no worse for her experiences.

"*Darf ich jetzt zu ihr sitzen?*" I asked the reception officer, who was now locking the door behind us. I didn't want her to be alone.

Frau Werner answered. "Yes, you should go over to her now.

The interview will begin any moment."

As if they had been waiting for her cue, two men emerged from the office door behind the desk where Shin sat. The first was a short, heavyset Japanese man. He was conversing in rapid German with a blond police officer of similar height and stature. When they reached Shin's chair, she stood at once and bowed low to both. All three of them had seated themselves around the desk by the time I joined them, but Shin leapt up again in surprise when she saw me. "Ree-yong!" Clearly still nervous, she managed a smile that did my heart good. The translator glanced at the blond officer, who gave him a subtle nod.

Frau Werner dragged a chair over from a nearby desk and sat on my other side. That made sense, I thought. Her job was working with foreigners, and a plaque on the blond officer's desk read *Ausländerbüro.* Office of Foreigners. Plus Frau Werner had already proven she had a close relationship with the police. All of a sudden I was very glad she had come.

The Japanese man laid an open ledger on the corner of the desk, settled a pair of round spectacles on his nose, and uncapped a silver fountain pen. "*Hajimemashou ka? O-namae wa?*"

Shin bowed her head as she spoke. "*Shin Oon-Myung. Kankoku-jin desu.*"

The translator's pen hovered over his ledger. He gave the blond officer another sidelong glance. "*Jouzu ni nihongo wo hanaserun desu ne.*"

She bowed again. "*Watashi no sobo ga oshiete kuremashita.*"

He finally began to scratch some notes, writing vertically down the right side of the page. A few minutes into the interview Shin took my hand and began kneading it distractedly as she spoke. She seemed to focus her massage on the same points where she stuck the needles in her acupuncture treatments. I became so entranced with the strong, sure movements of her fingers that I was shocked when I looked up to see shiny tear tracks on her cheeks. She was speaking evenly, making no effort to wipe the tears from her face.

At last the translator capped his pen and rattled off the facts Shin had shared with him with the blond officer. His clipped, heavily accented German was infuriatingly difficult to understand, but the German officer and Frau Werner hung on his every word. After he finished he excused himself to the office behind the desk.

Frau Werner clicked her tongue. "*Armes Ding.*"

I understood these words: *Poor thing.* The blond officer nodded his agreement.

"What'd he say?" I asked Frau Werner. "I couldn't understand a thing."

"Your friend has had a very difficult experience in St. Goar," she said sadly.

"She's not a prostitute," I said, the words seemingly forced from my mouth.

"Not a prostitute," Frau Werner said. I let out a breath I hadn't realized I'd been holding. "I believe the English term is 'mail-order bride.'"

My hand jerked involuntarily out of Shin's. "She's married?" Then the full implication hit me. "She's married to the muscle guy?"

"*Er heißt Jens Rammstein,*" the blond officer added helpfully.

Frau Werner nodded. "Yes, Herr Rammstein told the police he selected your friend from an online catalogue of East Asian mail-order brides. He apparently believed her skill in acupuncture would give him an edge in his strength competitions."

My head was shaking as if with palsy. "Wait, you already knew this?"

"I did not want to tell you anything until we had interviewed your friend, in case Herr Rammstein's statements disagreed with hers. However, they both tell the same story."

"But…"

I looked helplessly around the station. The other police officers and workers continued going about their business as if the world were not ending right here in the middle of their building. I sat up straighter, fighting for control. "But that doesn't make sense. Why would she leave Japan to marry some guy she didn't even know?"

"*Südkorea,*" the officer supplied in that same helpful tone.

"What?"

"She is from South Korea, not Japan," said Frau Werner. "Apparently she learned Japanese from her grandmother. The translator said she speaks quite well."

"She's not Japanese?" I repeated hollowly. Somehow this bit of news felt even more devastating than Shin's marriage.

Gentle fingers touched my arm. "Ree-yong?"

I twitched, unable to look at her. "What else did she say?" Although I didn't much want to hear the answer, I doubted any of it could make me feel worse than I already did.

Frau Werner squinted as if attempting to mentally organize everything the translator had told them. "She was raised by her grandmother in Seoul, South Korea. She has no other family since her parents were killed in an automobile accident when she was twenty-one."

"When she was twenty-one?" I interrupted. "How old is she now?"

"*Achtundzwanzig?*" Frau Werner asked the blond officer. He nodded.

Twenty-eight. Ten years older than I was. And I'd originally guessed she might be a year or two younger. I was starting to feel angry with Shin now, as if she had been lying to me since we met.

"A couple of years ago," Frau Werner went on, "her grandmother developed cancer. South Korea has a universal health care system similar to ours, but from what your friend says, it is inefficient in dealing with long-term illnesses. She and her grandmother spent nearly all of their money on hospital treatments. Then there came a point when she could no longer work as an acupuncturist because she needed to care for her grandmother at home."

"So, if she had to take care of her grandma at home, why'd she come here?"

Frau Werner frowned. "Can you not guess? They were in desperate need of money and, as I explained to you the other day, Germany is a very lucrative marketplace for sexual commerce. The mail-order bride industry is also strong. Especially so for a woman with your friend's unique skills. Herr Rammstein offered her two hundred thousand Euros to come to Germany to be his wife and acupuncturist."

I felt dirty, tainted. Each of the tiny pinpricks on my hand seemed to burn like pockmarks from some shameful disease.

"She used the last of her money to book passage to Germany," Frau Werner continued relentlessly. Her voice had hardened. "However, Herr Rammstein did not intend to pay her until after his next competition. He claimed their agreement would only be fulfilled after her treatments had proven advantageous to his career. When she realized what was happening, she refused to give him any more treatments. He became violent. She attacked him and fled, eventually locating shelter in the Abbey of Saint Anthony, where you discovered her soon after."

Frau Werner broke into another of her rare smiles. "It seems you were correct—you were able to find a service assignment after all. One that is more important by far than anything I could have arranged for you."

Was she mocking me? I glared at a spot on the floor between my shoes.

The office door clicked open behind us. The translator came around the desk and sat down wearing a grim expression. Shin's small, icy hand found mine again and this time I let her take it.

"*Zannen desu ga,*" the translator said heavily. "*Shin-san no o-baa-san ga o-nakunari ni narimashita.*"

Shin's chest heaved three times as she took in his words. Suddenly she loosed a keening wail that raised the hair on my neck and arms. I didn't need a translation of his message. Her grandmother must have died.

Shin slid forward out of her chair and would have knocked her head against the corner of the desk if I had not caught her. The others around the desk stood instinctively. Shin clung to me, desperate sobs wracking her body so hard that we both swayed. Several people in the station had stopped working to stare.

This continued until the blond officer moved over to Frau Werner and whispered urgently in her ear. She laid a hand on my shoulder. "Leon, they need to speak with Shin privately."

Shin, still gasping, allowed herself to be shepherded into the office behind us. "So now what happens? Will she be deported or something?"

Frau Werner shook her head helplessly. "It will take some time to work out the legal matter of her residency."

"Her home is in Korea," I said.

Frau Werner blinked. "Her grandmother has died."

"Yeah, I understood that much. But they had a house or something, right?"

"Shin was her grandmother's only surviving family member. No one was able to contact her after her grandmother's death. Their property now belongs to the government. There is nothing for Shin back home."

"Well she can't stay here."

Frau Werner was watching me with a very peculiar expression. "Herr Rammstein claims he filed the necessary paperwork to allow your friend to stay in Germany, although since their marriage has been dissolved…" She shook her head again. "At the very least she can remain at the Hotel Schwarzer Bär until these matters are cleared up. Perhaps I can find some money in our budget to cover her room for a night or two." She sighed. "Regardless, she may need to remain here at the station overnight. You will return for her in the morning? I can pay your ferry passage."

I nodded, barely listening. More than anything I wanted to be out of the station, away from everyone. I turned without another word and walked to the steel door that led to the lobby. The reception officer opened it for me.

Autumn, Elise, and Bernie were waiting in a knot by the stand of brochures. They launched into a litany of interrogatives the moment I came through the door:

"What happened?"

"Where's Shin?"

"Is she okay?"

I ignored their questions. "I need to call my mom. Do any of you have a phone card?" They only watched me. "I'll pay you back."

Bernie pulled a plastic wallet from his pocket and slid what looked like a credit card out of it. "Just type the number on the back of the card and then your home number."

"Thanks."

Outside, the sun seemed especially bright and hot after the station's cool interior. There was a single payphone mounted in the sidewalk a few paces away from the entrance. I lifted the receiver, which was almost too hot to touch, and dialed the numbers as Bernie had instructed.

Mom answered on the first ring. "Leon?"

"Hi, Mom," I said blankly. Conflicting emotions were crashing and roaring through every inch of my body but I refused to feel any of them. "I'm sorry I hung up on you before."

"No, I'm the one who should apologize," she gushed. "I shouldn't have threatened to bring you home. Mrs. Werner explained to me how much you have done for that Japanese girl. What's her name? Shin-something?"

"South Korean," I said, and now some bitterness did creep into my voice. I suppressed it. None of this was Shin's fault. "There's one more thing I have to do for her, and I was thinking our church back home could help with a fund raiser or something. It's for a good cause."

I could tell Mom was surprised by this but she seemed determined to keep the conversation civil. "What do you want us to do?"

I heard Frau Werner's voice as clearly as if she were standing beside me: *There is nothing for Shin back home.* But I suppressed that too. There was even less for her in St. Goar.

"We need to help Shin get home. She needs to go back to South Korea."

DISC 4

1

I spoke to my mother for another ten minutes. In addition to hammering out details about the fundraiser I hoped the church would perform, Mom questioned me at length about Germany, my host parents, and the other students on the trip, although she bravely kept the conversation away from Autumn. When we hung up I felt better, calmer, than I had at any time today.

I had a purpose again.

Autumn, Elise, and Bernie had given me my space while I was on the telephone, but they fell expectantly silent when I returned. Their expressions were anxious but eager, as if they could see my new purpose as clearly as I felt it.

"So?" Autumn said.

I returned Bernie's phone card. "Shin is still answering questions inside. But the good news is she's going home soon."

"Back to Japan?" Bernie said, sliding the card into his plastic wallet.

"South Korea."

"Then she's not Japanese?" Autumn asked, eyebrow cocked.

I knew what that look was about. Autumn hadn't been as quick to assume Shin's nationality as I had, but then again, she'd had no evidence that Shin wasn't Japanese. It didn't matter now anyway. If I was completely honest with myself, it hadn't mattered before either. Thinking otherwise had been my first mistake.

"She lived in Seoul with her grandmother—who taught her to speak Japanese," I added pointedly when Autumn's eyebrow rose still further.

"Does that mean she's okay?" Elise asked. "If they're letting her go home?"

"Yes, she's fine, thank goodness."

"That's wonderful," Elise beamed.

"When's she coming out?" Autumn asked.

"Tomorrow," I said. "I'm supposed to pick her up in the morning."

"Why?"

I shrugged. "Search me. Frau Werner said they want to keep her overnight."

This seemed to upset Autumn for some reason, but she headed back toward the pier with the rest of us. A return ferry to St. Goar idled lazily at the end of a long boardwalk. Elise and Bernie headed into the air conditioned cabin for lemonade.

"First round is on me if you want to join us," Bernie announced magnanimously. "A little get-out-of-jail celebration seems in order."

"No thanks. We'll find seats on the upper deck again."

Bernie shrugged. "It's your party." A blast of cool air washed over us as he slid open the cabin door.

The ferry's massive engines growled to life, causing the ferry's windows to rattle in their frames. I grabbed the stairway bannister one hand to steady myself, but before I could take the first step, someone had taken my other hand. Unlike Shin's had been in the station, this new grip was warm and strong.

"Hang on a second," It was Autumn. "That stuff you told us—

is that all you found out back there?"

I sighed, but Autumn wouldn't be satisfied until she had heard every detail of Shin's story for herself. And, truthfully, she had a right to hear it. Once we were seated on the upper deck, I relayed everything I had heard in the police station. Autumn listened in rapt, horrified silence.

"And because of all that," I finished, "I asked Mom if the church would help raise money to send Shin back to South Korea."

"What?" Autumn gasped. "How can you—"

"Germany has been hell for her," I said quietly.

"Which is why she needs a support system. We may not be her real family, but—"

"Do you think she would rather stay here and eat pretzels with random strangers or go home to rebuild her life? One that she understands."

"It sounds like that's why she left Korea in the first place," Autumn argued. "It's not up to you to decide where she goes next."

"The new life was for her grandmother, not her. And grandma's not part of the equation anymore, is she?"

"Listen to yourself!" Autumn said, sounding rather hysterical. "You are not a heartless person, Leon, so quit talking like one."

"Look, Shin isn't some lost little kid. She's ten years older than we are. She knows the ugliness of the world better than either of us ever will if we're lucky. I'm not going to make her life worse by forcing her to stay with me like some stray pet."

"No, you're going to toss her aside because she doesn't fit your weird game fantasy anymore."

I stared at her, nonplussed.

She colored. "I wasn't going to say anything because it seemed to be your main coping mechanism here in Germany, but I looked up *Endless Saga* at an internet café when I left you and Shin at the hospital the other day."

"Why—" I began, but my vocal cords seemed to have seized.

"It was so important to you. I…" Her cheeks were positively maroon now. "You said your game meant a lot to you, so I thought I should look it up. To be a good friend."

Heat was beginning to rise in my own cheeks. "To be a good friend," I repeated.

She cleared her throat, looking slightly confused but determined. "Your little catchphrase—'I would have done the same for anyone'—that's from your game. The fact that you called Shin 'Salvia' when we found her, how you told her she was 'alive,' even the way you kissed her while you were hiding from that group of guys. Those things all happened in your video game. All of them."

A new fire was kindling in my chest. "So you're spying on me now?"

"What? No, I—"

"Not spying? Then what was it? Were you doing scientific research about delusional people? Or, I know, you were going to pretend to like video games because you're madly in love with me. That must be it."

"Don't…" She turned away and stared fixedly down at her lap, the shining curtain of her hair only partially obscuring her face, which had turned the color of a boiled lobster.

"Hang on," I said.

She looked up hopefully. But she must not have been encouraged by my expression because she turned away again immediately.

"Mom was right. You really do only know one way to relate to boys, don't you?"

She sat mutely, head bowed, hands folded in her lap like a penitent nun. For some reason her silence only made me angrier, the flame in my chest leaping like a bonfire.

"It was fine being your friend," I said, "but you couldn't honestly have expected it to be more than that. Not with…"

She stood abruptly and walked toward the stairway leading to the lower deck. She paused on the top step and turned to face me again. The river breeze lifted her hair in a golden halo while her powerful legs flexed with the rolling movements of the ferry. Her eyes, as intelligent and brilliantly green as ever, regarded me with haughty new coldness.

That new intense bonfire of righteous indignation was snuffed out in an instant. I waited for her to speak, to annihilate me with whatever perfect retort she was packing in her psychological arsenal.

She smiled as if she knew precisely what I was thinking. That smile made me want to leap over the railing and swim for the opposite shore, but I was pinned to the bench, paralyzed.

Without a word she turned her back on me and marched down the steps, out of sight.

2

Bernie was waiting at the end of the dock when I disembarked from the ferry in St. Goar. Autumn and Elise were nowhere to be seen. "How was your lemonade?" I asked cautiously.

He gave me a stoic thumbs up. "Smooth."

Had Autumn told him about our argument or was this just more of Bernie being strange? "The girls already leave?"

"Yessir. I think they were going to stop at the greenhouse to see about their work schedules tomorrow. But I'm heading home. You want to walk together as far as the *Marktplatz*?"

I jabbed a thumb to the south. "My place is on the river, just a couple blocks that way."

"Oh, that's right. Frau Werner gave me a little map of where everyone lives. Well, have a good one, I guess."

He spun around and started west, toward the center of town.

"Wait! You, uh, want to come hang out? My host parents won't care."

He paused and checked his watch. "I'd better not. It's already after four and I promised I'd be home for dinner at five."

"Is it really that late?"

It seemed impossible that so much of the day had slipped away. Yet this morning also seemed like a lifetime ago. When I considered that I had woken up only a few hours ago fretting that I had kissed Shin, only to be interrupted by Autumn bursting into my room in her flimsy nightshirt to tell me about the different ways men behave hatefully to women...

"—morrow?" Bernie was asking.

"Sorry?"

"I said, do you want to hang out tomorrow? The kindergarten where I work won't open until next week because of this flu thing. We could nab some quality dude time, maybe play a little *Endless Saga.*"

I wondered again how much Autumn had told him and Elise. But then I remembered he'd seen me start up his game outside Frau Werner's office. I relaxed. "I should probably stick around home so Frau Werner can call to tell me when to pick up Shin."

"No prob, Bob. I'll just pop over after breakfast." He renewed his easy pace up the sidewalk and waved carelessly over his shoulder. "Schwartzendruber out."

I watched him go, feeling oddly panicked. The calm that had followed the telephone call with my mother had long since been shredded in the walking maelstrom of emotions that was Autumn, and the prospect of a whole evening with only my thoughts to keep me company seemed grim indeed.

Which is probably why, thirty minutes later, I was sitting cross legged on the hard futon in my bedroom, firing up Bernie's Gamicon to play *Endless Saga.* Frau Werner must have told Greta what had happened today because at some point she offered to bring food up to my room like she'd done the morning after I got my stitches. This time I took her up on the offer. I simply couldn't face the idea of being crammed next to Autumn at that tiny kitchen table for an entire meal, pretending nothing had gone wrong between us while her leg brushed against mine under the table.

Autumn surprisingly did not try to enter my room, although I heard her come upstairs after dinner. She seemed to pause in the hallway and for a second I tensed, finger on the Gamicon's pause button, but then her door creaked open and shut and she made no more sounds.

Aside from those few interruptions, *Endless Saga* served its purpose admirably. I remembered thanking Greta when she set the tray of food inside my door, seeing the steam rise off the boiled potatoes and ham. I even remembered smelling it—the sauerkraut was especially aromatic in the small room. But when I slid off the futon a few minutes later, or so I thought, the whole plate was stone cold. In one moment the rectangular patch of sky visible through the skylight glowed a deep red as if the whole world were on fire. The next I saw only a flat dark rectangle like a blackboard cut into the ceiling.

When I at last set the Gamicon aside, hands pregnant with the promise of deep ache in the morning, I elected not to check the clock. I simply slid on my gloves, put out the light, and collapsed for the second night in a row into a series of troubled dreams.

The one I remembered this time ended with me in a graveyard, wielding Typhoon Darkwater's fiery Combustion Sword against a horde of shadowy figures. I danced and swung, carving an effortless path through my enemies until only one remained. I kicked out, catching the last figure in the gut so that it flew backward, arms pinwheeling uselessly, into an open grave plot. Flickering flames from my sword lit the figure's face as it fell and I saw, without surprise, Shin's agonized face. Her dark eyes watched me until the lip of the grave separated us. I launched myself forward to catch her, sick with fear, but too late. She thudded into an empty wooden casket, the lid of which swung ponderously down and sealed itself with a crash. Shin's fists beat piteously, almost delicately, against the inside of the casket.

The sound of her feeble rapping carried on even as the dream faded and my brightly lit bedroom resolved around me.

"*Kind? Bist du schon aufgewacht?*" Greta's voice. She was knocking on the bedroom door.

My eyes flicked to the travel alarm, which read 10:04. I struggled to extricate myself from the bed sheet, which clung to my sweating body. The sun shone directly through the skylight and the temperature in my room seemed to be about a hundred degrees.

"*Dein Freund ist da,*" Greta reported.

"*Danke!*" I called, at last freeing myself from the sheet and jamming my legs into the first pair of shorts I lifted out of the growing clothes pile on the floor.

Two minutes later I skidded down the last few steps into the kitchen, where Bernie and Greta sat chatting serenely. Before him were plates of bread and cheese and a steaming mug of coffee.

"Welcome," Bernie said. He gestured politely to one of the empty chairs, inviting me to sit as if I were visiting his house instead of the other way around.

"Yeah, sorry. Have you been here a long time?"

"Few minutes," he said.

Greta stood, beaming at him—she must have found his German up to scratch as they'd conversed while waiting for me—and busied herself at the counter.

"*Entschuldigung,*" I apologized to her.

"*Ja, ja. Kinder verschlafen immer.*"

"So what are we doing today?" Bernie asked, rubbing his hands together. "Video games?" He glanced at my hands. I was still wearing my gloves. "Or not. What about the cinema? My cousin told me that instead of previews, German theaters play thirty minutes of cigarette commercials before they start the actual movie. Wouldn't that be weird?"

"Weird," I agreed. "But I need to stay here and wait for Frau Werner to call, remember? I'm supposed to pick up Shin this morning."

Bernie took a sip of coffee and smacked his lips in apparent enjoyment. "Nah, you're off the hook. Autumn went to bring her back to St. Goar while you were asleep. Your host mom was just telling me."

"Oh," I said, completely taken aback.

Greta set another plate in front of me. I began eating mechanically, not really tasting the food.

"So?" Bernie prompted.

"So…" I responded, eyebrows raised. "What?"

"A whole day of dude time awaits us. What are we going to do with it?"

3

It turned out the European power adaptor was only one of the many electronic cords and cables Bernie had brought with him to Germany. With Greta's permission, he connected his Gamicon Lite to the television in the living room and we spent the next several hours of our "dude time" playing *Endless Saga* on the big screen. Actually, Bernie played while I watched, occasionally giving him pointers on how to level up more quickly or access secret areas in the game world.

I had never played a video game with someone before and I found the experience enjoyable but somehow indecent, as if he and I were participating in one another's private fantasies. Undoubtedly Autumn would be able to explain...

But thinking about Autumn was too disturbing. After only a few days of knowing her, she had already become the closest thing to a best friend that I'd ever had. And yet, learning she liked me had changed something, flipped some switch in my brain that made me see her differently.

She had said I didn't treat her the way boys normally did, and the same was true of her. No girl besides my mother had ever paid so much attention to me.

Which led to what Mom had said about Autumn and all "girls like her." Was it true that Autumn didn't know how to be friends with a guy without making it romantic? Did that mean that she only paid attention to me because she liked me, or had she only started liking me after we spent so much time together?

It wasn't like she'd ever tried any funny business with me. Certainly she was immodest about her body compared to most of the girls in New Canaan but that didn't translate into making a pass. No, I was the one who had forced myself on an unwilling partner.

"Bernie, have you ever kissed a girl?" I asked suddenly.

Bernie's eyes never left the screen. "Sure, lots of times."

I sat forward. "Really? Like, a girl girl? I don't mean kissing your mom on the cheek."

"A girl girl," he confirmed. "My special lady and I like to mess it up sometimes. It's nice."

An idiotic grin was spreading across my face. Surely this was more of Bernie's special brand of nonsense. "What's her name?"

"You'll laugh."

"Why? What's her name?"

"Bernice."

I burst out laughing.

"See?" he said unperturbedly. "But love is blind to the names of those it enslaves. What about you?"

"Me what?"

"You ever kiss anyone?"

My smile faded. "Once. It didn't go very well."

Bernie nodded sagely. "The first time I tried to get fresh with Bernice we were watching a movie. This one really funny scene broke us both up so bad we could hardly breathe. That was the first time I knew I loved her, so I kissed her. She was still laughing and I kissed her full on the teeth but she didn't mind."

"She didn't?" I asked, fascinated. And suddenly, unexpectedly, I found myself describing what had happened between Shin and me in that darkened bakery entrance after we left the pizza party.

"That's awkward," Bernie laughed. "You really should have known better."

I glared at the side of his head. He still didn't turn away from the TV. Finally I asked, "What do you mean?"

"There's nothing between you two. No snap!" He took his hand off the controller and snapped his fingers. "No crackle, no pop. Now, if you'd pulled that same stunt with Autumn..."

"If *anyone* pulled that stunt with Autumn..." I muttered. Unable to stop myself, I added, "She only knows one way to relate to boys."

"Ah," Bernie said with an air of just having solved a mystery. "You guys are fighting. I wondered what was going on when Autumn and Elise scrammed so quickly from the dock yesterday."

I could think of nothing to say to this. On the television screen, Typhoon Darkwater took a running leap from the wing of an exploding airship and landed safely on the back of his robotic winged horse, Mechasus.

Bernie shrugged. "You know Autumn better than I do, of course. But I can't see her responding very well if Hat or I tried it on with her. Not that I would," he added with a comradely nod in my direction, eyes still on the screen. "Hat did, though, didn't he? Over and over at the pizza restaurant. Distasteful."

"He bought her pictures."

"So did my brothers," Bernie said with another shrug. "They're very alluring pictures. But a photo is separate from a person, fictional. Somehow I don't think Autumn would like my brothers slavering all over her in real life any more than she liked Hat doing it."

So Bernie's brothers also owned the Different Seasons photos, did they? I imagined them, two hulking farm boys, faces blue and goblin-like in the glow of a computer screen, leering at Autumn's body. It was Shin's husband and his friend all over again, the way they had made squeezing motions at Autumn the other night in the bar as if she were a sex doll.

"Now compare her reaction to Hat at the restaurant to the moment you showed up at the ice cream place yesterday," Bernie continued. "The sparks flying between you two almost melted our ice cream."

I remembered what he was talking about but I didn't quite share his interpretation. "We're friends," I explained. "All this stuff with Shin has just brought us closer together. You know, that thing about a shared crisis making a relationship stronger."

"Bitch, please. If you'd never met Shin, you and Autumn would probably be engaged by now. I expect a front row seat at the wedding ceremony, by the way. Or I would if I didn't hate weddings so much."

For several seconds the only sound was the clicking of buttons on the Gamicon. On the television, Typhoon Darkwater and Mechasus swooped down through the retractable roof of their forest headquarters. Salvia came pelting out of the control room and leapt into his arms.

Bernie pointed at the screen. "Is it my imagination or does that girl look exactly like Shin?"

I watched the two characters on the screen clutch each other, Salvia weeping with relief at his return and Typhoon Darkwater stroking her hair. I'd viewed this scene more times than I could remember but this was the first time the characters struck me as appearing inhuman, like marionettes operated by gifted puppeteers.

"Pure imagination," I said. All of a sudden I needed to talk to Autumn very badly.

But she still had not returned by supper. Greta invited Bernie to stay, charmed that he spoke to her only in German. He attempted to decline but Klaus shouted him down, clearly as intrigued as his wife with Bernie's presence, though he spoke English with Bernie as he did with Autumn and me.

The telephone rang at the end of the meal as Greta was serving everyone a thick square of multi-layered chocolate cake for dessert.

"*Ist das Autumn gewesen?*" I asked when Greta returned to the table. She shook her head.

"Leon is very concerned that the Autumn is still away, yes?" Klaus informed Bernie, winking over his third bottle of beer. "They are never without each other, *verstehst du?*"

"Inseparable," Bernie agreed, raising his mineral water in a formal toast.

I couldn't decide whether to laugh or give Bernie the evil eye for encouraging Klaus. Greta rattled off a couple sentences I barely understood, owing either to unfamiliar vocabulary or the fact that she had consumed two glasses of red wine with dinner.

"My Gretelchen says there is magic in the walls of this house!" Klaus roared happily. "It brings true love to any who live here." He reached across the table to pat her affectionately on the cheek. She blushed and gave his hand a coquettish little smack.

Bernie beamed at them. "We should all be so lucky."

I wolfed the rest of my cake, not wishing to be trapped at the table while Klaus and Greta became progressively sappier. Bernie seemed to take the hint and we were able to excuse ourselves a few minutes later, thanking my host parents repeatedly as we backed out of the kitchen.

At the door Bernie heaved his backpack onto his shoulders with a weary grunt. "You coming too?"

"Yes," I said. "As far as the *Marktplatz.*"

Bernie smirked at this but said nothing as we headed outside. A block away, the river sparked and waved with the same fierce red-orange hues as the setting sun. All across town, peaked roofs and angular brown and white *Fachwerk* threw deep shadows across the houses they adorned.

"I bet if I tried to take a picture right now it would turn out like crap," Bernie said. He immediately slid his backpack to the sidewalk and rooted through it until he found his digital camera, which he aimed at me. "Say 'alpine fire,'" he said.

"What?"

He snapped the picture and stared at the little screen until my face came up. "Nice one!" he hooted.

We covered the rest of the short distance to the *Marktplatz* in amiable conversation about Klaus and Greta, whom Bernie considered to be pleasant hosts and top notch entertainers. Neither of us mentioned Autumn or Shin, though he walked with me all the way to the entrance of the Hotel Schwarzer Bär.

"Thanks for coming over today. I had a lot of fun."

He held out his hand, which I shook. "We simply must do this again."

"You got it. Next time maybe you can introduce me to your host parents."

"Rainer and Silke," he said, nodding. "Or, as I call them, Cornwallis and Yvette. See you later."

"See you."

Bernie strolled off into the growing dark. Without turning back he called, "Good luck!"

4

The familiar gentleman with the flyaway eyebrows came lumbering out of the office behind the front desk and waved in greeting when he recognized me. I pointed wordlessly up the stairs as I walked toward them.

"*Ja, ja,*" he said pleasantly, already retreating into his office. "*Die Mädchen sind oben.*"

I took the stairs two at a time. I knew what I had to tell Autumn and how difficult it might be, but at the same time I felt more excitement than dread. My day with Bernie, while strange and occasionally awkward, seemed to have ejected some of the emotional baggage I'd woken up with this morning.

Autumn opened the door after the first knock. For a second she looked like she wanted to close the door again but she stepped back so I could come inside. The room was full of the sound of running water.

"Shin's in the shower," Autumn said, indicating the closed bathroom door. She sat down on the bed. "We visited the castle today." The implied end of the sentence—"without you"—hung in the air between us like poisonous mist. "How about you?"

"Bernie came over. We hung out, played some *Endless Saga*."

"Did you?" Her face wore that same terrifying expression from the ferry, the one that said she could destroy me with a word.

"You were completely right," I said. "About me, the game, Shin, everything." I hesitated. Here came the hard part. "And that's exactly why she has to go back to Korea."

She flared up at once, opening her mouth to argue. I held up a hand. "Please. This whole time I've been trying to improve her situation, to save her from it. I got so angry in the police station when I heard all of the things that had happened to Shin."

"Well it's all awful."

"The thing is, I was angry *at* her, not for her."

"What do you mean?"

"It's exactly what you said earlier—she didn't fit my game fantasy anymore. I'd had this idea that God dropped Shin in St. Goar so I could solve all her problems, defeat her enemies, and ride off into a beautiful moonrise on a space-boat, happily ever after."

"Is this you trying to make sense?" she asked acidly.

"When the translator in the police station told Shin her grandmother had died, she collapsed against me like something inside her had died too. And all of a sudden, just like that, the bubble popped. I couldn't deny that Shin was anything but a real person with terrible, overwhelming problems. And that made *me* the character living in an imaginary game world. It was…" I cast around for the right word. "Unnerving."

For once Autumn seemed to have nothing to say. The trickle of water in the bathroom ceased. Shin must have been getting out of the shower.

I spoke more quickly, hoping to hash all this out before Shin came back into the room. "So you were right when you accused me of wanting to send Shin back to Korea because of the game, but for the opposite reason. I'm not trying to send her home because she broke out of my game fantasy, I'm trying to send her home because I put her into that fantasy to begin with. Her life here, however terrible it was, only got worse because of me."

A familiar, shrewd look had crept across Autumn's face. I knew she was looking for signs of self-pity or evasion. I also knew she wouldn't see those things because they weren't there.

"Are you going to tell Shin about this?" she finally asked.

"What, about the video game?"

"That you're going to send her back to Korea. You said it yourself, she's not a little kid. Shouldn't she have the right to choose where she lives? It's not like she has a house or job to go back to in Korea."

"You think I would put her on an airplane and just forget about her?" I said indignantly. "Mom is going to try to raise enough money at church for Shin's travel expenses plus a couple thousand dollars to help her get back on her feet."

The bathroom door creaked open. Shin stepped through wearing a white robe with the Hotel Schwarzer Bär logo embroidered over the breast. "Ree-yong," she said, smiling vaguely. She must have heard my voice from the bathroom because she didn't seem surprised to see me.

"Well," Autumn said brusquely. "I still think Shin has a right to know what you've decided about her future."

"Be my guest," I said, becoming annoyed now. I'd felt so certain that Autumn would come around if I explained myself adequately but she seemed determined to fight. "Your Korean is as good as mine."

Autumn scooted over and patted the space beside her on the bed. "Sweetie?"

Shin sat down. Now that I saw her more closely her eyes were puffy, as if she'd been crying in the shower. She seemed to have developed worry lines around her nose and mouth in the last twenty-four hours. For the first time I could believe she was almost thirty years old.

"You're in Germany now," Autumn said gently. She gestured all around the room, then pointed to the floor. "Germany, right?"

Shin seemed to pull herself together. She nodded.

Autumn nodded back encouragingly. "And Leon would like to give you money—" Autumn mimed passing over several bills like a bank teller cashing a check. "—to go back to South Korea." Autumn made a long arc through the air with her hand made a *zzhhh* noise like a toddler providing sound effects for a toy jet.

"With some extra money," I added. "For the plane ticket—" I repeated Autumn's bank teller and airplane gestures. "—and for you." I pointed at her and pretended to pass over another stack of bills.

Shin looked back and forth between us, her expression eloquently miserable, then she nodded again. "Sankyew."

It was a moment before I realized she was saying, in English, "Thank you."

"You're welcome," I said reflexively.

She stood and padded over to her dresser and pulled the little gold box of needles from the top drawer before returning to her spot beside Autumn. She held out the box like a gift.

Autumn didn't take the box. "Leon, what is she doing?"

"I don't know."

Shin now turned up toward me, her expression as purposeful as I had seen it since the first time she had treated my hands back in the hospital room. Just like she had done then, she reached for my hand. "*Igot juseyo.*"

I nearly refused. Those needles had been used on her husband too, and who knew what drugs or diseases were coursing through his body? Then again, if some blood borne ailment was going to pass from him to me it had almost certainly done so already.

Besides that, the treatments worked. I could use my hands again.

I dragged the room's only chair out from under a little writing desk in the corner, set it in front of the bed, and sat. Shin raised the gold box between me and Autumn so we could both see it. She traced the raised red markings on the top it as if reading Braille.

"*Nampyeongwa anae.*"

Autumn nodded encouragingly. "Your needles? Acupuncture?"

Shin shook her head. "*Otto to tsuma.*" She was watching me, eyebrows raised.

"Hazubando," she said carefully to me. Then, indicating Autumn, "Waifu." She traced the raised symbols with a ragged fingernail, held up two fingers, then took Autumn's and my hands and placed them, one on top of the other, on the gold box.

"Hap-py," she finished, satisfied with the identical shade of pink we had both turned. Releasing us, she set the box aside and told Autumn in a much more businesslike tone, "*Sigye.*"

For the next hour, the two of them held, prodded, and squeezed my hands over and over until Shin seemed satisfied Autumn could find all of the pressure points from my wrist downward. I paid close attention too, curious about why Shin wasn't simply teaching me to do it myself. But it quickly became apparent that treating some of the points most effectively meant touching more than one at the same time, which required two free hands. She only used two needles in the whole process, inserting one herself and allowing Autumn to do the other, presumably to show her how deeply they should penetrate the skin.

"Did that hurt?" Autumn asked when Shin excused herself to wash the used needles in the bathroom.

I shook my head. The truth was that Autumn had never hurt my hands, although she had touched them more than anyone besides my doctor, my mother, or Shin.

Before I could comment on this Shin returned from the bathroom and once again raised the gold box delicately, almost reverently to Autumn. "Hap-py," she repeated.

Autumn hesitated, looking as helpless as I'd ever seen her, but in the end she accepted the box. She didn't seem able to speak.

Shin bowed bowed low to each of us. "Sankyew," she said to me. "Sankyew," she said to Autumn.

Autumn stood and we each copied her uncertainly. Then, before Autumn had straightened up completely, she rushed forward and enveloped Shin in a tight hug. "I'm so sorry about your grandma."

Shin accepted the hug and returned it as awkwardly as we had bowed to her.

"We'll see you tomorrow, okay?" I said.

She bobbed her head once, smiling despite her obvious exhaustion. "*Jago sip-eoyo,*" she said, indicating her bed.

"Sleep good," Autumn said.

Shin tilted her head at us as if studying a painting that was hanging crooked. Then she grabbed both of us by the wrist and brought our hands together.

Autumn's fingers slid into mine, warm and strong and sure.

"*Deo,*" Shin said, smiling again, and opened the door for us to leave.

5

Outside the hotel, the *Marktplatz* hummed and clattered with its evening crowd of diners, tourists, and German workers walking home for the night. The sun had finally dropped behind Burg Rheinfels, and in the harsh ghost lighting that shone across its entire length like stage lights, the castle looked every bit the grim fortress that had once commanded this stretch of the river. The silver disc of the moon hung above, bright and hugely magnified in the humid valley air.

Autumn walked silently beside me, both hands clasping the gold box of needles between her breasts as if it were a child that required comforting. Was she worrying that Shin had passed the needles—and with them, the implied responsibility for my hands—to her? Because however Autumn might feel about me, such a vast responsibility couldn't seem very appealing to an eighteen year old girl.

"Look, you don't have to—" I began, reaching for the box.

Autumn's whole body jerked away from me and she collided with an older German woman.

"*Pass auf, Kind,*" the woman reprimanded stiffly.

Autumn seemed not to notice. Her eyes, always so expressive, were wide and hurt and terrified.

"Oh no," I said, realizing what my gesture must have looked like. "I wasn't going to touch your—I only meant—"

But she didn't seem to hear me any more than she had heard the German woman. "Something was very messed up back there, Leon." She held up the box. "Why did she give me this?"

I frowned. It seemed obvious to me but I didn't want to say so. Not when Autumn was clearly so distraught. "She doesn't need them anymore," I said gently. "She probably brought them as a gift for her husband and now she's not with him anymore. I bet she doesn't want anything that will remind her of her time in Germany. Would you?"

We were standing at the edge of a crosswalk. People were piling up behind us. I reached for Autumn's hand. She allowed herself to be pulled into motion.

"You don't have to keep working on my hands," I said when we had reached the opposite sidewalk. "I mean, it was really nice of you to take that box. I'm sure it made Shin feel better. But who knows how often you and I will see each other after this summer."

She withdrew her hand from mine and brought it back up to the box, which she clasped against her chest once more.

"I'm sorry I said that thing yesterday about how you relate to boys. I was still angry from what had happened in the police station and I couldn't believe you actually—"

But Autumn had stopped walking again. "You've already forgotten about her."

"What?"

"She's not Japanese, she's not Salvia from your game, so she's not your friend."

"My fr—" I began, outraged. "Did you not hear anything I said back there? You've told me and showed me how pathetic I am sometimes, so why don't you let me learn from those mistakes and let Shin try to carve out a normal life for herself?"

But once again Autumn seemed not to be listening. She was craning her neck back toward the *Marktplatz* as if expecting to see Shin following us like a homeless puppy. None of this was going at all how I had imagined.

I forced myself to calm down. "Shin can take care of herself."

At these words Autumn suddenly became herself again. She nodded decisively and handed me the gold box. "You hold this, I don't have any pockets. We're going back to make sure."

"Make sure of what?" I said, accepting the box and sliding it into the cargo pocket of my shorts.

"That she's okay," Autumn said.

She turned to set off but I didn't move. "I'm telling you, I thought about this all last night and all day today. We'll do what we can for her but Shin doesn't need us."

"We'll see," Autumn said. "Let's go."

"Shin deserves her privacy," I said stubbornly.

Autumn continued to back away from me toward the *Markt-platz*, beckoning for me to follow. But I thought I understood this. Here, finally, was the passive aggressive behavior I'd seen so often growing up.

"Okay, have fun," I said, turning in the opposite direction. "See you back home."

Without warning Autumn's hands fell on my shoulders. She spun me around, grabbed my t-shirt in both hands and kissed me hard on the mouth. Before I could do more than flail my arms for balance it was over and she was staring forcefully into my eyes, our faces inches apart. Bright spots of color were blooming high on her cheeks but these were not marks of embarrassment. In that moment she looked more vibrantly alive than anyone or anything I had ever seen in my life.

"I had no right to call you pathetic, Leon. You are as close to a hero as humanity ever gets. Come with me now or don't. Nothing will change my mind about you."

My heart was drumming so hard and so high in my throat that I honestly wondered whether I might be having a heart attack. A worryingly pleasant numbness was spreading downward from my stomach. My hands were shaking. I grabbed Autumn's shoulders partly to keep my balance and partly because I wanted to touch her bare arms.

"You did that on purpose," I said.

She didn't look remotely abashed. "And it worked, right? You're coming back with me."

"Yes."

"Good. How's that for knowing how to relate to boys?"

But she didn't pull away immediately. I was afraid of how much I wanted her to kiss me again and much more afraid of how much she wanted to. Her breath was coming in hot little blasts like steam from an engine. I thought I finally understood what Bernie had meant about the sparks between Autumn and me being able to melt ice cream.

At last she drew away, shaking her head as if to clear it. "Okay, maybe it wasn't completely on purpose."

I laughed. It was a bizarre, high titter that sounded like it should have come from a small jungle animal. It was not the sort of sound a hero would ever make. I jammed my hands in my pockets so Autumn wouldn't see how badly they were still shaking.

"Do you really think something is wrong with Shin?" I asked.

"Yeah. I really think so."

"Okay. Let's go back."

We turned and walked together toward the thronging *Marktplatz,* not talking, not daring to touch, and unaware of anyone besides each other.

6

The Hotel Schwarzer Bär's clerk greeted us kindly enough when we reentered the lobby, though his wild eyebrows knitted in surprise. Autumn was already heading toward the narrow staircase to Shin's room when he said, "*Ihre Freundin ist nicht da.*"

"What?" Autumn said, pausing with her leg on the first step. However, something in her expression suggested that for once she understood the man's German perfectly.

He said, "*Sie hat das Hotel gerade verlassen. Möchten Sie den Zimmerschlüssel?*"

"Where did she—" Autumn began, but caught herself. "*Wo ist sie gehen?*"

I didn't bother to correct her grammar. The numbness had returned to my stomach, no longer pleasant in the slightest.

The clerk shrugged. "*Sie ist zwei Minuten nach Euch aus dem Hotel gegangen. Vielleicht hat sie Hunger. Sie ist jedenfalls sehr dünn, nicht wahr?*"

"What?" Autumn repeated, and this time it was clear she hadn't understood.

"She left a couple minutes after we did. He doesn't know where. *Danke*," I told him.

"Shit," Autumn said under her breath as we passed yet again through the hotel doors onto the *Marktplatz*. "Shit."

"Where would she have gone?"

"The where doesn't worry me nearly as much as the why," Autumn said, climbing onto one of the decorative shrubbery cribs outside the hotel and peering uselessly over the crowd. Shin could have been ten feet away and Autumn probably wouldn't have located her among the much taller Germans.

"You don't think she's gone looking for her husband, do you? For revenge or something?"

Autumn leapt down from the shrubbery. "No, Leon, I think she's going to kill herself."

"That's not funny."

"It's not supposed to be funny," she said. "God, why did we leave her alone?"

"Just stop," I said, pulling her to a halt and studying her face carefully. "You're serious, aren't you? You really think she wants to commit suicide."

"I should have known the instant she gave me that box. She even taught me how to do the whole acupuncture thing on your hands. God *damn* it, I never thought she'd leave her room to do it. Maybe she didn't want us to be the ones to find her."

Whether I actually believed Autumn or had simply caught her hysteria, an image swam into my mind of Shin standing at the edge of the cliffs near the Abbey of St. Anthony, black hair whipping around her face in the updraft from the river as she tipped forward, plummeted fifty feet and shattered her body against the rocks below.

But, I realized, if Shin wanted to do herself in, why would she bother to go all the way out to the cliffs when the Abbey itself offered so many mortal dangers, from barbed wire to collapsing walls to sharp bits of wood and metal?

This time my brain conjured a picture of Shin lying in the center of the bombed out abbey, impaled on a rusty spear of rebar, twitching and weeping her final tears...

Get a hold of yourself, I thought savagely. If Autumn was right, panicking would do Shin no good. And besides, there was no real evidence Autumn was right, so there was no reason to panic. Not yet.

Autumn was watching me, waiting for me to act. For me to be the hero. It was a ludicrous idea but it somehow calmed me down a little.

"Okay. Last time Shin ran away she went to the abbey. That's where we should start."

"She didn't just run away—" Autumn began desperately.

"It's a place she knows," I insisted. "And if you're right about what she's doing, where better to do it than the abbey? We both know that place is a deathtrap even if you're not trying to..."

The sentence hung unfinished, feeling much more real than it had any right to feel. We turned south together and began walking toward the edge of town. The problem was, after a minute walking didn't seem nearly fast enough. So we started jogging.

It's the panic, I told myself. *Running will only make it worse.*

But very soon jogging wasn't fast enough either, and we were both running. My legs were longer but Autumn was in better shape and soon she was ahead of me. I pushed harder and drew alongside her. I remembered Autumn checking her guidebook after we'd discovered Shin in the abbey ruins, saying the town square was less than a mile from the abbey. However, as we ran the distance seemed to stretch to an infinity of burning lungs and mindless terror.

Voices and pictures roared through my mind in a torrent as ragged as my own breathing: Shin's expression of misery when we explained that she would be returning to South Korea; Frau Werner telling me, *There is nothing for Shin back home;* Autumn's self-chastisement for not realizing, the moment she received the gold box, that Shin planned to kill herself; Shin's despairing wail when she heard her grandmother had passed away.

That's when I should have known, I realized.

Still more came: Shin's appearance in the abbey's ancient wooden doorframe before falling down the steps into the grass; the tense, stiff feel of her body the night I kissed her; her shrieks echoing through the street yesterday morning as her husband carried her away.

Amid this onslaught of memory rose a single, terrible idea: death could not possibly seem worse to Shin than her life in Germany had been.

Autumn and I charged into the tall, swaying grasses that separated the southernmost real estate of St. Goar from the long fields that ended in cliffs at the river. The grass rippled and swayed in the silver moonlight like seaweed on the ocean floor.

"Do you...see her?" Autumn panted, hands resting on her knees.

"No," I gasped. Air whistled in my throat and I tasted something like metal on the back of my tongue.

Without another word we took off again, thundering across the hilltop where we had eaten lunch our first day here, a lifetime ago. The ground tilted downward to reveal the abbey ruins with its loose assortment of scattered rubble and solitary pillars like claws. The hand of death itself, perhaps, reaching up through the old bombing ground to drag down one more life.

But surely, a final, rational vestige of my mind pleaded, such thinking was asinine, panic-induced nonsense. Autumn and I were close enough to the abbey now that if Shin were actually in there she would be visible by moonlight.

"What..." Autumn shouted. "What is she doing?"

I squinted ahead. There was someone, an indistinct figure

standing in the empty, leaning doorframe where we'd first seen Shin. But the person looked too tall. He or she seemed to be wrapping something around the top of the wooden frame, which was at least eight feet off the ground.

Ahead of me, Autumn leaped the barbed wire fence and kept running. I had just enough time to adjust my already uneven stride to attempt the jump. But I was tired. The toe of my sneaker clipped the top wire and suddenly I was flying horizontally through the air. I managed to twist my body so that my shoulder hit the ground first and I rolled three times before leaping up and charging after Autumn again.

Autumn didn't seem to have noticed me falling and, with a jolt that almost sent me sprawling again, I realized why. The person in the doorway *was* Shin. She was facing away from us, balanced on a wobbly rectangular stone she must have hauled into place by herself. In the time it had taken me to fall and regain my feet, she had finished whatever she'd been doing to the top of the doorframe. Now she seemed to be winding something around her neck.

Autumn was screaming, or maybe it was me. We were still fifty feet away. Much too far. Shin's hands dropped to her sides. She shifted her balance. The wobbly stone supporting her tipped and thudded down the steps.

The cord around her neck seemed to stretch or slide a few inches, and for a moment I dared to hope. Surely the cord would break. I could see it glinting in the moonlight. It looked extremely thin—definitely not thick enough to support a grown person, even one as slender as Shin.

But the cord did hold, and Shin's feet continued to dance and thrash as if unaware they had nothing left to stand on.

7

Shin could not have been suspended for more than five seconds before Autumn reached her but as I pounded across the empty grass toward her, wind gusting in my lungs and ears like a storm at high tide, time stretched impossibly. I seemed to be running through water or perhaps molasses and it felt as if each stride brought me no closer to her. It wasn't possible—we simply couldn't be this close and still be too late.

Time ground back into gear the moment Autumn leapt up the low stone steps into the doorway. She crouched, put her head between Shin's dangling legs, and hoisted Shin's body into the air. But she stood too high and cracked Shin's head on the bottom of the wooden doorframe. Shin began to slide sideways on Autumn's shoulders.

"Leon!"

Then I was beside her, supporting Shin's upper body while Autumn continued to bear her weight, bent awkwardly to hold Shin's head high enough so she wouldn't strangle but low enough so that her head wouldn't hit the door again.

"How is she?" Autumn gasped. "Is she okay?"

I shook my head, too winded to speak. Shin was still alive, I could see that right away, but far from okay. Her eyes rolled like those of a spooked horse and her complexion was both ashy and too dark. Blood trickled from below the dark, thin bands wound around her neck...

"Oh God." The words were ripped out of my throat as if by a fish hook so that I couldn't tell whether they were a prayer or an oath.

Autumn's head snapped up. "What is it? What, Leon, talk to me!"

"She used barbed wire."

"What?"

"She hanged herself with barbed wire. She must have picked up a loose piece of it over by the fence."

"Get it off her!"

I fumbled unsuccessfully at her neck. For once my fingers weren't the problem. The wire had been wrapped at least five times, with the final rotations burying the first one against the skin. Worse still, in those few seconds when the wire had borne all of her weight, it had tightened to the point that Shin would certainly suffocate whether Autumn continued to hold her or not. And there wasn't enough play in the wire even now to unwrap it without the barbs slicing Shin's face to ribbons.

My eyes followed the wire up to the door frame, where it had been wrapped at least twice as many times as it had been around her neck. The frame itself looked unstable, rickety...

"I'm going to try to knock it over," I said.

"Knock what over?" Autumn asked in alarm.

I jumped onto the cracked stones to the left of the doorway. My stitches were burning with sweat and my shoulder still throbbed where I had fallen but now was not the time to worry about minor discomforts. I leaned against the wooden pillar, braced my legs on the stones, and heaved with all my strength. The frame shook very slightly. Dust drifted from the ancient seams to be whisked away on the wind. I heaved again and again but the frame didn't move any more than it had the first time.

"Whatever you're doing, do it faster," Autumn called. "She's slipping again. I think she's blacking out."

"It's no good, I can't push it over. I'll have to unwind the wire from the wood."

Without waiting for an answer I started climbing up the thick wooden beams onto the frame. It took my weight with ease. I should have realized right away I wouldn't be able to knock it down.

"Are you sure?" Autumn said, attempting to look up at me in her half-crouch. "What about your hands?"

"Never felt better," I said truthfully, crouching on the doorframe above the girls like a gargoyle. "You just hold her."

This end of the wire had obviously tightened too. There were raw scrapes in the wood where the wire had dug into it when Shin had stepped off her rock. But I was at least able to pick out the end of the wire and begin unwinding it from around the wood. A long barb here and there caught in the wood, but overall the wire came loose more easily than I could have hoped. The problem was that the last loop was the one that held Shin's head so close to the door frame. Otherwise I could have had her free by now.

Still, at this rate it would only take a few more seconds. "Just about there!" I called. "You ready?"

"Yes, hurry!"

I had unwound the wire down to the second-to-last turn when Shin slid almost completely off Autumn's shoulders. Under the influence of this new weight and inertia, the loose end of the wire I'd been working with whipped rapidly around and around the wooden frame like a helicopter blade and I was forced to stand up so the spinning wire wouldn't catch my face. Below me, I saw Autumn stagger backward toward the steps. She seemed to be keeping her feet. And the wire was loose. Shin was fr—

A loud squeal and a thunk came from from somewhere around my feet. Shin gave a desperate squawk.

I looked down and saw that a particularly long and sharp barb in the last loop of wire had buried itself in the wood like a nail. Down below, Autumn had somehow managed to keep her balance and hold Shin upright, but Shin wasn't free at all. The wire continued to bind her to the doorframe.

"What happened?" Autumn called. "Do you have it?"

I didn't waste time answering. The noise Shin had just made told me the wire was tighter than ever around her neck. Whatever meager air supply the wire had allowed her so far had certainly been cut off by that last jerk.

There was no time to think, no time to plan. I hunkered again, grabbed the wire in both hands, and pulled upward with every bit of strength I had in my body. One of the barbs punctured the thick pad of flesh on the outer edge of my palm, but I hardly felt it. The wire would come out. It had to.

I gave one final, frantic yank. The wood splintered as the barb came free. The soles of my shoes slipped forward as my body fell backward. The wire, now completely free from the doorframe, slashed in the opposite direction through my fingers with a jagged, silver lance of pain.

Time slowed down once more as I tipped backward into empty space. I had plenty of time to hear Autumn's shout of triumph: "You did it, Leon!" Plenty of time to watch wispy evening clouds scud across the dome of the sky as I fell away from it. Plenty of time to see the untethered wire whip out of sight over the doorframe like the tail of an angry dragon. Plenty of time to see two of my own fingers arc away from my left hand, trailing through the air after the wire.

Those fingers touched Autumn's arm after she kissed me, I realized. For some reason the idea made me very happy and very sad.

I was still waiting for my life to flash before my eyes when I hit the ground.

ENDING CINEMATIC

The bedroom door banged open. Before I even had a chance to sit up Autumn had charged into the room and jumped onto the end of my futon, blocking out the rays of morning sun glaring through the skylight. She was completely dressed, shoes and all. "Why aren't you up?" she demanded.

I checked my travel alarm, panicking slightly. It read 6:45. I flopped back and ground my palms against my eyes. "Why *are* you up?" I moaned. "We don't have to be at the airport until eleven."

"Couldn't sleep," Autumn said happily and dropped onto the bed cross-legged. She poked me in the side. "We're going home. Home!"

"I know—*ow!* Stop it. Okay, we're going home. Yay. Just quit poking me."

"Never," she said. "Come on, budge over."

I scooted over to the edge of the bed and Autumn reclined beside me. She had done this every single morning for the last two and a half months. In fact it was about the only time we saw each other alone anymore, considering that she worked at the greenhouse all day while I worked with Shin. All three of us typically spent our evenings with Bernie, Elise, and Hat, either in the *Marktplatz* or else at one of our host homes.

But ever since I had come back from my stay at the hospital up in Cologne at the end of our first week in St. Goar, Autumn had made sure we had this time together every morning.

I knew why. I didn't think I would ever forget laying amid the stones and sharp grass inside the abbey, wondering if I was paralyzed or would ever be able to breathe again, and seeing Autumn's face hover into view above me as she skidded through the empty doorway and fell to her knees beside me.

By mutual admission it had been the worst moment of both our lives. The blood spreading across my shirt from my missing fingers had momentarily convinced Autumn I was dead, and the expression of absolute terror and anguish on her face had told me that we'd been too slow to save Shin after all.

But then Autumn's eyes traveled up to my face and she realized I was looking back at her.

"We lost her," I said. The words came in a dusty croak.

Autumn leaned closer. Her hair hung down in a silk curtain and tickled my cheeks. A tear dripped from the tip of her nose onto mine. "What'd you say, baby?"

"We didn't save Shin."

But Autumn was smiling. She gently tilted my head forward so that I could see Shin propped against the stone wall. Her face looked swollen and a band of dark, irritated skin ran along her jawline. She was coughing fitfully, very clearly alive.

Autumn grunted as she lifted me into a sitting position. "I'm going for help. Will you two be okay?"

Without waiting for an answer she turned to Shin. "I'll be back as quickly as I can. You take care of him."

An understanding seemed to pass between them. Shin bobbed

her head with some difficulty—that particular movement would likely be painful for a few days at least—and crawled over to where I sat. She took my left hand and lifted it above my head to stem the flow of blood as I leaned backward against her chest. She was making hoarse vocalizations that sounded like moans of pain. As they grew stronger, changing in length and pitch, I understood she was singing. It sounded like a lullaby. I wondered if it was something her grandmother had sung to her.

Autumn returned in what felt like a very short amount of time, accompanied by two large blond men in bright red jumpsuits. They carried a stretcher and a large first-aid kit.

"How'd you get back so fast?" I asked, struggling and failing to sit up on my own steam.

"I called them from the first house I got to," she said.

I groaned. "Why didn't we think of that last time?"

One paramedic treated Shin's neck while the other bound my left hand in so much gauze it looked like I was wearing a boxing glove. To my surprise they put me on the stretcher rather than Shin. I heard one of them mutter to the other, in German, something about a back fracture.

But it turned out that my back had been fine, as had everything besides my left hand. Now, lying on my futon, I flexed the fingers that had been briefly separated from the rest of me. The ring finger and pinkie were still stiff, but I could move them.

During the ambulance ride to Cologne that night I had decided in my delirium that two fingers were a more than reasonable price to pay for Shin's life. But a ten-hour surgery, nearly three months of physical therapy, and, of course, daily acupuncture treatments from Shin had slowly returned the use of those fingers. Even my arthritis had faded back into a dull hum that I really only noticed in the morning and evening or in particularly humid weather.

"Do you have all the paperwork done?" Autumn asked now, staring up through the skylight in my room.

"The most important thing is Shin's work visa—that thing Frau Werner got in the mail from the consulate at the end of last week. She still can't believe we turned around an H1B visa in two months. Although," I suddenly remembered, "get this. Just yesterday I found out from the chiropractor in New Canaan that Shin can start training there the Monday after we get back. How about that?"

"Oh," Autumn said. "And Shin's house will be ready for sure?"

I sat up, frowning. It wasn't like Autumn to ask questions to which she already knew the answer. "It's been ready for a couple weeks. I gave you that newspaper clipping Mom sent. Didn't you read it?"

At the end of July someone at the church had placed in the offering plate an unmarked envelope that contained the deed to a little rundown house on the edge of town. The youth group had spent a whole weekend repainting and decorating the place with donated furniture. The place had been for sale for years and Dad suspected someone from the bank had quietly unloaded the property for tax reasons, whatever that meant. But the youth group had done a nice job fixing it up and a house was a house. And Shin had been over the moon about it when I'd shown her pictures.

Autumn sat up now too. "Can we still hang out sometimes when we get back to Iowa?"

"I sure hope so," I began, steeling myself. Now was as good a time as any to tell her what I'd done.

"You were right about Shin," Autumn said, almost too quietly to hear. "I don't know if it was God, but something made sure you two would be in St. Goar this summer."

"What are you talking about?"

"Your arthritis is gone, you speak Korean. Shin's got papers, a place to live, and now a job with the chiropractor? It was meant to be. It's so obvious."

She stood abruptly and left the room. She called from the hallway between our rooms, "Breakfast in ten."

I sat, stunned, for several seconds. I had learned some Korean, that was true. Frau Werner had picked up a German-Korean phrasebook in Cologne so Shin and I could communicate better as we tried to figure out where she should go next.

It seemed Frau Werner had been right about there being nothing left for Shin in Korea. Shortly after we had started using the phrasebook, Shin had discovered a phrase that she immediately pointed out to me: *Korea ist nicht mehr meine Heimat.* Or, in English, *Korea is no longer my homeland.*

This single sentence had led me to start researching methods of immigration to the US. Frau Werner had pointed me toward H1B documentation for specialized workers. Shin's acupuncture practice hadn't been able to keep up with her grandmother's hospital bills, which was why she'd come to Germany in the first place, but a licensed acupuncturist certainly qualified as a specialized worker. The chiropractor in New Canaan seemed to agree with me.

And in the meantime Shin and I had enjoyed simple conversations in Korean. But they were artless, silly things on my part. I mostly kept them up because Shin giggled at my accent and each day I could make her laugh felt like a day she wouldn't try to kill herself again.

She told me about her grandmother and I told her, in absurdly broken phrases from the book, about my family and New Canaan. She had seemed very excited about the town, especially after I first managed to communicate that she could come home with Autumn and me instead of returning to Korea if she wanted to.

Nowhere in these conversations had Shin expressed any interest in being in romantic relationship with me. Or with anyone else, for that matter. I had a definite sense that old Jens Rammstein, Shin's erstwhile husband, had soured her on men for a long, long time. And even if she had been interested, well, it was like Bernie had said. The instant I'd ditched the fantasy about *Endless Saga* I had realized for myself that Shin and I would never be more than good friends. No snap, crackle, or pop. No sparks that could melt ice cream.

I snatched my trusty cargo shorts and a t-shirt off the floor and dressed hastily. I never should have let this go on for so long.

Greta's face and silver hair popped into view at the bottom of the staircase when I stepped into the hallway. "*Fünf Minuten noch. Dann gibt's Müsli.*"

"*Danke,*" I called distractedly, striding across the hall to Autumn's room.

The door hung slightly ajar. Although I'd never been in her room before I only gave a single knock and pushed through without waiting for an answer. Unlike my room, in which the only window was the large skylight set into the slanted ceiling, the entire north wall of Autumn's room was windows. If not for the house next door she would have had an excellent view of the *Marktplatz* cathedral and Rheinfels Castle.

Autumn was sitting on the edge of her bed and when I came in she jumped so violently she almost fell off. Her eyes were red and puffy. "Don't you knock? God." She irritably swiped a tissue from a box beside her bed and blew her nose.

My mouth had gone very dry. Was I really about to do this? I took a deep breath. "This has been the best summer of my life."

Autumn stared blankly at me, a fresh tissue in her hand. "Well, I'm glad that's settled. Don't forget to close the door on your w—"

"And I've never thanked you for being so cool to me."

She fell back and sighed theatrically at the ceiling. "I knew I shouldn't have come over to see you this morning. I'm already emotional about going home."

I licked my lips. I should have gotten a glass of water from Greta before coming in here. Oh well, too late. "You're my best friend."

Without sitting up, Autumn said, "That's cool, I'll make us matching bracelets."

"Do you know why I worked so hard to make sure everything

would be in order for Shin before we left Germany? I wanted to make sure you and I would have more time to be together when we get back to New Canaan."

Now she did sit up, staring incredulously as if giving me time to take back the dumb thing I'd just said. When I failed to do so, she said, "You realize that I see you two together every day, right? You think I didn't notice her little Korean pet name for you? *Dong-saeng*," she added in a surprisingly good imitation of Shin's accent.

"That word means little brother," I said. "Look, my favorite part of every day is when you come wake me up."

"Don't make this harder for me," she said. Her lip was trembling again. "You and I had a great time this summer but we both know we won't see each other again after we go home."

"We won't?"

She made a frustrated noise and actually stamped her foot. "You are such an idiot sometimes. How thrilled do you think your mom and your dad would be to introduce me at church? 'And this is Leon's girlfriend, the internet porn star.'"

"I don't think they even know about—"

"I lied to you," she said desperately. "After my Different Seasons site went live I bought banner ads on a couple social networking sites. Thought I may as well do the thing right."

"I doubt my parents saw—"

"Don't you get it? I didn't sell four thousand pictures, I sold four *hundred* thousand. In less than two days. I panicked completely and pulled the ads and shut down my site but the money was already in my account. It took me a month just to print all the pictures and shipping labels and send them out."

My eyes bugged as my brain performed the math. And then something else clicked into place. "*You* donated the house. You asked your dad to put the deed in the offering plate, right?"

"My mom, actually," she said miserably. "She's less recognizable in New Canaan and you weren't ever supposed to know about it."

"But why? It's great! Shin loves the house. She'll be so pumped that you—"

"There was never any chance I'd be able to pull all my pictures off the internet but I thought if I could just take down the ones with my real name on them…"

Neither of us said anything. My brain seemed on the verge of shutdown in the wake of all this new information.

"Girls like me don't get to be with guys like you. I should have known that from the beginning."

"Now who's being pathetic?" I said, trying to make a joke. She flinched as if I'd slapped her.

I crossed the room and knelt in front of the bed. "I've been trying to figure out how you could keep visiting me every morning when we get back to Iowa."

"Oh, well I imagine your mother would leave the pet door unlocked for me," she said scathingly. "Give her a call and ask if I can pop in for breakfast. See what she says."

"She says that'll be fine." Which was perfectly true. She had been surprisingly accepting when I told her on the telephone that I wanted to continue seeing Autumn after I returned home. Although I elected not to share my suspicion with Autumn that Mom had simply been humoring me, saving the real discussion until I got back to Iowa.

Autumn glared at me. "What are you talking about?"

"You remember when I called her yesterday to tell her our flight schedule? I also told her you were going to be coming around every day. Or," I added, "I can come to your place. Doesn't matter to me."

She looked horrorstruck. "Why?"

"I knew it was the only thing that would convince you I'm serious. Shin's cool and everything, but she's not you. She never was."

"But your parents—"

"Will deal with it," I said firmly. "And if they don't I'll move out."

"You told your mom that?"

"Yes." Attempting another joke, I added, "Maybe some beautiful philanthropist will take pity and buy me a house too."

Autumn rolled her eyes and thudded dramatically backward onto the bed.

"I've never been anyone's boyfriend and frankly I don't know or care whether that's what I am to you. I mean, I know we haven't…" I reddened. "Been physical since that first time and that's okay."

"I wanted to prove I knew other ways to relate to boys," she told the ceiling. I wasn't sure whether she was kidding or not.

"That was a stupid thing for my mom to say and even stupider when I said it. What she thinks of us is none of our business."

Autumn emitted a strangled sound that might have been a laugh or a sob.

"The only thing I want is to keep seeing you when we go home. You…you're my favorite," I finished lamely. She covered her face with her hands and said nothing. After a minute of this I rose awkwardly to my feet. "I just wanted to say that."

My hand was on the doorknob when I heard the bed creak behind me. Before I could turn around Autumn flattened me against the door, which quaked on its hinges.

"*Alles in Ordnung?*" Greta called up the stairs in alarm.

"We're fine!" I called breathlessly. Autumn was squeezing me so hard I thought my ribs might crack. "Just let me loose so I can hug you back," I told her, laughing.

She did, but only long enough for me to turn around. Then she threw herself at me again, standing on tiptoe, burying her face in my neck. "You're my favorite too," she whispered.

I don't know how long we stood that way. We were very late for breakfast.

ABOUT ST. GOAR

Some of my more well-traveled readers may realize that I have taken great liberty with the geography of the Rhine River Valley. Although there really is a town called St. Goar with an old castle called Burg Rheinfels near the famous Lorelei, the St. Goar portrayed in this book is pure fiction—an amalgamation of several beautiful German towns on the Rhine as viewed through the dusty window of memory. If any readers out there would like to see an updated version of this book with a more factual version of St. Goar, I would be happy to accept funding for a research trip. I think a month of travel expenses would about do the trick.

ACKNOWLEDGMENTS

This book would not have been possible without the help of some very able and patient people. First, as always, I must thank my wife, Kate. Without her support none of my books would exist, and that is particularly true for this one.

I also owe a permanent debt to Alan Rinzler for imparting two invaluable skills any writer must possess: first, the tools to tell a compelling story (if the story on the preceding pages was not compelling to you, the fault is mine); and second, the ability to learn from criticism.

Next, thanks must go to my able language experts Sabine Holzheu, Naoko Takahashi, and Andrea Voogd for help with German, Japanese, and Korean respectively. Once again, any remaining mistakes in usage are mine. Many other generous folks played roles as test readers for this book too, and I want to give particular thanks to Hope, Christian, Hannah, Keith, Matthew, Benji and Susie. Thanks also to Juliet Ulman for her editing insights early in the project.

Final thanks go to you for reading this book. Come back as often as you like.

ABOUT THE AUTHOR

André Swartley lives in southern Japan with his wife and son. He likes video games almost as much as Leon Martin does.

CPSIA information can be obtained at www.ICGtesting.com
Printed in the USA
LVOW01s1204021113

359719LV00005B/728/P